Wings of

Discovery

"The story and characters are fictional.
The lessons on life and flying are real."

by
Captain Stacey L. Chance

Llumina Press

ISBN: 1-932047-09-3

Printed in the United States of America

Acknowledgments

For the most part this story is a work of fiction. The aviation and weather related content is based on fact and is accurate to the best of my knowledge. The thrust for *Wings of Discovery* grew out of a groundswell of emails. During the summer of 2001 I started an interactive online fear of flying course to help nervous airline passengers. The feedback from my students provided me with a better understanding of how and why flying gives so many people the jitters. The reaction I have received from my course graduates motivated me to write *Wings*.

I would like to first thank those I thought I was helping, my *Fear of Flying Help Course* students. But it was they who showed me a passenger's most common concerns and misconceptions about flying. I would also like to express my gratitude to Patricia O'Brien for her generous and skilled assistance with this project. She acted as my creative consultant, editor, and project cheerleader. Thanks to Rob Csongor for the fine photo on the cover. My family also deserves credit for displaying great patience with me during this time. A thank you should also go out to some of my good friends whose "uniqueness" helped inspire the novelty found in the book's characters.

I hope you enjoy the adventure and learn something along the way. Now please fasten your seatbelt and place your tray table in the upright position...

Table of Contents

Chapter 1
White Knuckles

*H*er highlighted hair is neatly pulled back and she wears a crisp white uniform blouse tucked into a regulation length navy blue skirt. An attractive woman in her early thirties, she appears unfazed by our circumstances. She's clearly a professional; experienced, knowledgeable, and obviously trained in life saving techniques. Calmly making her way down the aisle, she wears a businesslike expression that says, "Please don't bother me unless it's important." How does she maintain her composure in the middle of this chaos? Doesn't she realize the certain danger we face?

Suddenly my seat shudders and shakes. I instinctively brace for the worst and the rumbling beneath me fuels a gasp of shock. Outside my window strange flickers of light split the darkness with odd horizontal lines. Is it rain, hail, or snow streaking by? Just as I take a deep breath to get a grip on my fear we abruptly drop. My drink sloshes and threatens to spill as the horrible sensation of free fall shoots my stomach up into my throat. How can I get rid of this soda? Maybe the flight attendant will be back to collect our drinks before my shirt gets stained. But is it really safe for her to be up and about? A quick glance reveals that she doesn't look concerned in the least. Her easy smile and pleasant conversation with a woman up the aisle does nothing to ease my gnawing fear.

I make an effort to appear relaxed despite my feeling our lives are in jeopardy. Like any ordinary person I want to feel in control of my fate. I tell myself that fear is natural when facing the unknown or when feeling threatened. In spite of efforts to rationalize my feelings, panic begins to surface. My mind fights to stay in charge, but my body's natural defense mechanism kicks into high gear. My head reels, and my stomach churns as my hands become cold and clammy. I can't catch my breath, and as my heart races faster a new worry escalates. Am I going to pass out, have a heart attack, or lose control altogether?

Minutes pass before I realize the plane has stabilized. With a sigh, I close my eyes and try to catch my breath. I don't understand these feelings and fears. As an educated forty three year old, I shouldn't be frightened. I've always been able to handle difficult situations with poise, and now I can't seem to keep anxiety from setting in. Feeling miserable, I'm embarrassed by my failure to maintain even basic self-control.

A couple of sharp jolts cause the wings to bounce and flex, testing the plane's structure. Perspiration beads on my forehead. The engines growl and surge, and my hands flex and clench in response. I do not belong here. This is a mistake. Why do we choose to hurtle through the stratosphere in large metal tubes? I should never have stepped foot onto this plane.

Stuck in my mind are the haunting words that played on the radio as I drove to the airport. *"Bye, bye Miss American Pie... this will be the day that I die, this will be the day that I die."* I'm not usually superstitious, but now I'm worried the lyrics may be prophetic. People say Don McLean's song is about fifty's music, and how it has changed since Buddy Holly's untimely death; a young life cut short by a...plane crash!

It occurs to me this would be an especially unfortunate coincidence. My mind is cluttered with morbid thoughts of looming disaster. My greatest fear is turbulence and each bump and drop sends me closer to the edge of self control. Will a large air pocket cause a wing to shed? With just one wing the plane would surely spin out of control as the pilots hopelessly struggle to upright the crippled ship. Plunging at ever greater speeds, the death spiral would generate terrifying screams from all aboard. As we are pressed deeper into our seats under the accelerating forces, the airframe would creak and groan from the tremendous strain. People and objects would be tossed crazily about the cabin.

I imagine the plane auguring earthward. Time would slow to an agonizing pace as we collectively ponder our horrifying and unavoidable demise. Twisting down … down … down. What will that last fraction of a second feel like? Our nightmare would abruptly end in a deafening crash, followed by an intense firestorm engulfing the impact crater and surrounding landscape. The next morning's headlines would brazenly shout out the death toll in huge bold type.

"Ding!" In a cold sweat and numb with fear, I am jolted back to the present to see that the seatbelt sign is illuminated. Then the indistinct drawl of the pilot sounds over the garbled PA system as I strain to listen for an explanation.

"Well ladies and gentlemen; it looks as if we're entering an area of a little bumpiness as we fly through some of these rain showers. I've turned on the seatbelt sign. So for your own safety we ask that you please return to your seats, and make sure your seatbelts are securely fastened."

This is a little bumpiness? We are pounding all over the sky, and the pilot only now turns on the seatbelt sign. How long has he been flying planes? We've got a damn cowboy driving this thing!

I struggle to calm down and recover my sanity. This is irrational. The trip started out routinely enough. Arriving at San Francisco International Airport late in the afternoon for my trip to Denver, I hoped for an uneventful flight. The security screening made me feel better about the improbability of a hijacking. I could see they were checking everyone carefully, and was relieved to know more flights now have air marshals on board. The 9/11 attacks have made passengers more aware, and I am comforted by the belief that they will no longer sit passively by while hijackers take control of a jetliner.

The plane was half full so the boarding process went smoothly. As I took my seat I considered what I'd recently read on a travel website. I learned there was really no safest seat on the plane. Apparently there are so many variables involved it would be hard to predict which seat would be the best in an accident.

The website discussed other seating considerations. It said you can reduce the sensation of motion by sitting over the wings, because you will be at the airplane's pivot point. Not surprisingly, the center seat is the least favorite seat on the plane because you may end up having armrest wars with your seat mates. I chose a window seat over the wing hoping to get a nap and a smooth ride; unfortunately I would get little of either.

After a short taxi to the runway, the beginning of the takeoff seemed normal. In the past I enjoyed the feeling of power and acceleration, but now a new cloud of dread surrounds me with every flight. As if to feed my fears, the nose of the plane rose too high. I felt a distinct dip just after we left the ground. It was as if the whole plane was going to tip over, but incredibly it managed to keep climbing. Next there was a series of strange whining and thumping noises which shook what little confidence I felt. How can something as massive as a jetliner even get off the ground?

Now an hour into my flight I'm a total wreck. I feel trapped, panicky, out of control, and self-conscious about my nervousness. A wild thought pops into my head, and I wonder how many passengers have had the uncontrollable urge to get up and scramble to the nearest exit to try to open the door in flight. Could others have such absurd ideas?

Several minutes pass without incident, and I begin to calm down. With rationality taking over, I now feel disgusted by my behavior. How had I, Mark Thomas, become such a fearful flier? I am a successful veterinarian with a thriving practice and wonderful family. How have I reached such a new low? This was supposed to be a simple weekend jaunt to my 25th high school reunion.

In my childhood I loved watching airplanes, and even dreamt of flight. I've flown many times as an adult, and experienced few problems. But recently the pressures of life have grown to nourish new anxieties. I've even experienced panic attacks in crowded places like busy malls and ball games. What's going on? Exactly where is this new vulnerability coming from? If I could identify the source at least I could try to change things. I guess as I get older the inevitability of my own mortality is starting to sink in. What will happen to my family when I'm gone?

Reflecting on my past I'm forced to recognize that fear is something I have a hard time admitting to anyone including my family. The last few years I have done my best to avoid air travel. When it was time to plan a vacation I always steered us away from flying in favor of road trips. My wife, Jennifer, would occasionally suggest jetting off to exotic destinations, but the thought of spending countless hours high above wide expanses of open water didn't particularly thrill me.

I decided Jennifer shouldn't go with me on this trip because our daughter, Shannon, shouldn't be left alone with the school year just starting. This decision was both a relief and a disappointment. It would have been good to have Jennifer come along, but I felt ashamed of the intensity of my fears. I just couldn't let Jennifer see me this way. I'm not sure which agonizes me more, the fear of flying, or the fear of fear!

In my eyes Jennifer hasn't changed much since I met her in college. A statuesque brown haired brown eyed beauty, she is spirited and smart. She felt self conscious about her height in high school, but by her early twenties, when I met her, she had filled out her tall frame quite nicely.

As we dated, her self confidence blossomed and she developed into a warm and compassionate mate. She is a great parent to our daughter; sensitive, yet firm; and always supportive of Shannon's adventures and interests. Even now I catch glimpses of Jennifer as the fun-loving impetuous college girl I fell in love with. The more comfortable she has become with herself, the more she is able to relax and display her playful spontaneous side. She is to me the embodiment of Van Morrison's song, "Brown Eyed Girl."

After spending years making sure my family and practice received the attention they needed, my own friendships suffered. Friends once important to me in school and early adulthood seemed to drift away. I thought this trip might do me good to see how some of my old buddies are getting along on our journey through life.

Finished with my soft drink I begin to relax. The cabin lights are low, and with the flight now smooth the passenger in front of me decides to take a nap. She reclines her seat confining me to an uncomfortably small area pinning my knees. Feeling a bit agitated I try to calm myself with the magazine in the seatback pocket. These airline magazines always seem bland. I begin to read an article on the Hawaiian Islands thinking this is a subject sure to quiet my mind. The page reads: "The lush green island of Kauai is one of the wettest spots on Earth. It averages more rain than the other islands of Hawaii; it is also called The Garden Island." I wonder if anyone ever says, "Hey honey let's book a flight to Kauai. We've got to get out of this sunshine. And make sure to pack the umbrella, this'll be fun!"

Looking out my window into the darkness I'm relieved that the flashes of light appear too regular to be lightening. It must be the plane's strobe lights. With each flash the streaks of raindrops appear frozen in time, but now they look larger. Has the rain gotten harder?

It doesn't take long for my anxiety to build once again. Straining to see if the droplets have grown I conclude they not only look larger, but they appear more densely packed. Oh no, here we go again! I put down my magazine, and speculate how much water a modern jet engine can consume without quitting.

Surely with heavy rain entering the engine the fire burning inside would be extinguished. First one, then soon the other engine would flame out as it struggles to maintain the jet's altitude. With both engines dead, and no generators to provide electricity or hydraulics, it would get awfully dark and quiet. I suppose the autopilot would soon click off, and the instruments would go blank. But that would hardly matter because the pilots would no longer have control of our aircraft.

Every poor soul on board would just be along for the ride, and a dark terrifying ride it would be. Without power to control the plane I picture it tipping over and dipping downward into the stormy night. Disappearing from radar the plane would begin a spiral towards the ground. As the plane turns and plummets in my mind, I imagine how my heart would beat harder and harder from the flood of adrenaline. Saying my prayers, I would reaffirm my love for my family. Pulsing and throbbing, the strong heart muscle would attempt to break free of its ribcage causing a massive...

"Snap out of it!" I shout to myself. How the hell did I go from the "Beautiful Hawaiian Islands" to my heart muscle exploding out of my chest at the precise moment of the plane's impact? I've got to get control of my imagination.

I recite to myself, "Get a grip! Get a grip!"

My feeble attempts to regain composure fail as my white knuckled hands involuntarily grasp the armrests in a subconscious attempt to keep the plane upright. A trickle of sweat snakes down my face and I wonder if technology is really worth the trouble. Desperately hanging on, I realize I have another hour and a half to ponder that question before we, God help us, finally land.

With a pleasant, but concerned smile the flight attendant approaches.

"Sir, excuse me, Sir? May I get you something else to drink?"

Interrupted from my private world of panic my eyes dart upward.

Chapter 2
The Encounter

*T*he Delta region of Central California is known for its fertile soil and acres of flat farmland. It has an elaborate system of irrigation taking advantage of miles of rivers, sloughs, and canals. The abundant water of the Delta is also enjoyed by boaters and other water sports enthusiasts.

Crops of tomatoes and corn are rotated throughout the year with corn being the most abundant produce. By late September many of the cornfields have been harvested leaving rows of dead yellow stalks. This time of year arguably has the best weather because the winds are light, and the temperatures are comfortably cooler than the summertime triple digit days. In a terrible melancholy mood I drive slowly home from Bill Garber's farm.

The trip to my high school reunion last week was a fiasco. Not only did I almost have a coronary on the flight, but none of the friends I hoped to see were there. The day after the reunion I cancelled my return flight out of anxiety. It was a long drive home, but at least I had plenty of time to think about things.

Mushrooming phobias are bad enough, and now my anxieties are compounded by this job. Feeling downcast, my arms weigh heavy as I cling to the steering wheel for support. As bad as I feel, I'm afraid Bill feels worse.

Bill owned Rusty for over fourteen years. Rusty was a good tempered intelligent dog with friendly eyes and a happy-go-lucky grin. Through all the years he was Bill's best friend and companion. He was special to me too, because as a puppy Rusty was one of the first patients at my clinic.

Owning an animal hospital has been a challenging experience. I have two nurses to assist me, and a receptionist to manage the schedule. Running the business side can be a chore, but the most difficult aspect of being a veterinarian is diagnosing the animals. We have many reliable techniques, but it would help if the animals could talk.

I have always loved animals. While growing up near Colorado Springs my family raised and trained guide dogs. My father taught Aviation History at the Air Force Academy, and in his free time he enjoyed restoring classic cars. Helping him work on those old cars taught me a lot about mechanical stuff, and the time we spent together was priceless. I showed a natural aptitude for machinery and my dad hoped I would become an airline mechanic or engineer; but my real interest was in animals.

After graduating from high school I enrolled at the University of California at Davis veterinary program located just west of Sacramento. I met Jennifer at the university, and after graduation we married and settled in a small farming town on the Delta. We found it to be a good place to have a family, and we liked the fact that we were only an hour's drive from the San Francisco Bay Area.

Normally I don't perform out-of-office euthanasia on Saturdays, but Bill had explained to me how Rusty had whimpered and cried all night. That poor old dog could hardly walk, and he suffered in constant pain. No matter how many times I have had to put someone's cherished pet down it is never easy. I try to be strong and supportive for the owner, but the experience is always emotionally draining.

Cruising along the narrow country road my thoughts begin to wander. Normally I'm a cheerful and optimistic person, but lately my world has grown dim with the feeling of walls closing in on me. Although I have little to complain about I'm in a rut. My options seem to dwindle as I get older.

I'm not sorry I chose the career I did, and I'm certainly not disappointed in my family, but my life is about half over now, and I feel like I'm missing out on something. As far as I know I'll only get one shot at living. Isn't it natural to want to assign more meaning to life? Surely others my age begin to look back, and wish they had done more, mattered more, or lived more?

We think we know so much. We think we have all the answers. Science and technology are great, but come up short. In my mind the biggest questions are still unanswered. Where did we come from? Where are we going? Is there a reason? What is life?

I don't go to church and prefer not to argue religion. I just don't care to have one particular faith confine my beliefs, and dictate how to interpret things. I'm not knocking church or religion, because I believe they contain many valuable lessons.

Can my fear of flying be helped through religion? Maybe a therapist can help with my fears? I prefer to solve my problems on my own because I believe if you look hard enough the answers will reveal themselves. It may not be obvious at first, but you just have to keep your eyes open.

I've always enjoyed music because it soothes my spirit and soul. Now about seven miles from home I pop in a CD. Jimmy Buffet sings "Cheeseburger in Paradise" on my truck's stereo. It does little for my mood, but starts my stomach growling for lunch.

As my truck rattles and shakes over some railroad tracks I'm reminded of that last plane ride. I figure if I were in flight an airline pilot would probably consider this: "a little area of bumpiness or light turbulence." My tire could easily have a blowout, and send me crashing into a ditch or oncoming traffic. Why am I such a nervous wreck on a plane, but hardly seem concerned about crashing my truck? Is it because the news media sensationalizes airplane crashes? Countless car accidents receive much less attention than plane crashes. Why is that?

Now with my window open to the outside air I try

hard to appreciate the day. The sun is warm, but without the scorching heat we received last month. Up ahead I notice a couple of birds flying in a curious way. My eyes aren't as sharp as they once were so I squint to see more clearly. The distant birds circle and pursue one another in a crazy and aggressive fashion. I have seen this before when one bird will chase another from a nest, but something is different about these particular birds. Nose to tail they hound each other unlike any birds I have observed. They are the same size and shape, but one is blue and the other green. Next they fly wing to wing performing playful swooping dives and graceful coordinated turns. High in the sky they dance and frolic for a time. Then spiraling and corkscrewing they glide downward to vanish in the distance behind a cornfield, never once flapping their wings.

Do birds fly and soar for fun? Do they value and appreciate their freedom? I thought they only flew for food and to flee their predators. What magically strange birds these must be!

I have heard inspiration is all around us, but our motivation must come from within. Witnessing this extraordinary display stimulates my fascination. If I was a bird I could be free of nagging worries and unbridled from gravity. To soar without boundaries and unfettered from fear, I too could find sanctuary from life's woes.

I feel a burden lift from my body, and no longer do I slouch in my seat. My mood mysteriously improves as I picture my life as a bird. I would never fear flying. A bird isn't concerned with turbulence, air pockets, or engines dying. They never worry about who's in control or if a wing will shed. Never does a bird feel claustrophobia or dread. Birds are fortunate to be free from the phobias I find so trying.

Relinquishing my worries I think ahead to my afternoon plans with my family. Far from the majority of houses, my road leads me past fields of tomatoes, freshly

14

plowed soil, and more corn. After a while off to the right I notice a flash of color in a sea of golden stalks. An unusual looking craft down one of the dirt roads catches my attention. Slowing for a better look, I watch as a tall figure walks to the edge of the road, and kneels down to gather round objects off the ground. Whatever he's doing is surely none of my business.

Glancing at my watch I gauge how much time it will take me to get home. I promised my family I would be back in time to take them to an afternoon movie. We always look forward to spending time together especially now that Shannon is so busy with school and work, and Jennifer is always on the go. Although they were disappointed when I told them about the house call, they understood. I should just go home, I thought as I continued to watch the odd figure stooping to pick up another round object.

With the intention of driving straight down the road my foot strangely eases off the accelerator, and onto the brakes. My hands turn the wheel to the right, and I veer off the pavement down the dirt road toward the strange vehicle. Why the heck did I do that, and why do I feel my life has also taken a new turn?

As I approach the unusual machine I recognize it as a small aircraft. Bright blue fabric covers the wings and tail. The body is bare, consisting of metal tubing and wire cables. Its engine is on top of the wing with the propeller behind. Low to the ground the cockpit sits out in the open, and has two low mounted side by side seats. A control stick is located between the seats, and two sets of rudder pedals are over the nose wheel.

Here before me is one of those "birds" I'd seen earlier. Its pilot is loading round green objects into one of the seats. I stop the truck, and prepare to get out when I am momentarily frozen by the sight of a second little plane. It emerges from behind the cornfield in a steeply banked turn.

This plane is similar to the first, but this one is green. Rolling wings level, it lines up on the road bearing down upon us. Through my windshield I see the blue plane and its pilot, and just beyond is the green plane growing rapidly in size as it approaches faster and faster! The sound of a tightly wound engine growls as the plane powers just a few feet above the dirt road kicking up swirling dust devils in its wake.

A nauseating bolt of dread forms in my stomach as I am certain to witness an awful mishap. I try to scream to the blue plane's pilot, but am paralyzed by fear. He casually piles the round objects into his seat oblivious to the danger. The green plane thrusts toward the parked plane, and with no room to spare it pulls up steeply just before impact. Leaning forward I see its wings flex from the terrific strain as the plane zooms skyward. Just as it loses its upward momentum the plane cascades over into a hammerhead turn. The motor becomes hushed as the plane smoothly glides around to settle gingerly on the road, coasting to rest a short distance away.

Relieved, I get out of my truck as the pilot of the green plane unfastens his seat belt, and takes off his headset. He is medium height with a happy round face and wavy brown hair. He is wearing sunglasses, jeans, and a t-shirt which reads: "UNITED FEDERATION OF PLANETS". Getting out of his seat he dashes over to the blue plane, and the two pilots begin an unusual banter all the while ignoring my presence.

Enthusiastic, the green plane's pilot calls out, "Hey Dan, I've got to reload. Wow! This stash of munitions you found is probably the best yet."

The pilot of the blue plane is tall and lanky with salt and pepper colored hair and a thick moustache. He has crow's feet around his eyes, a leathered face, and strong callused hands. Calmly pointing to the objects in his seat he smiles and says, "Yeah Rich check out these bunker busters. I bet these babies can penetrate reinforced armored plating."

"I scored a number of direct hits with my laser guided smart bombs on that rebel freighter. Then I followed up with a high altitude carpet bombing of their shipping channel." reports Rich, proudly raising his hand up in an animated gesture.

I inch cautiously closer. They must have seen me, but they act as if I'm invisible. What in the world are they talking about? Are they playing some sort of imaginary game?

"Good show!" Dan says. "You've got to take out those targets of opportunity when they present themselves. I'm reloading with some cluster bombs. Why don't you get set, and we'll go secure the perimeter. Then we'll head back to Dreamland, and see if Amelia wants to go for a ride."

Eyes beaming, Rich replies, "Good idea. I think she'd really enjoy that."

With each bizarre statement my curiosity grows. I suppose they're just up to some harmless fun, but I can't figure out exactly what they're doing. They act strange, but seem friendly enough. Throughout life I have found some of my best friends were the ones I had the most to learn from. Although many of my old friends are a bit unusual, I would probably find them dull if they behaved normally. Right away I feel a sort of kindred spirit with these two; they fit the mold of the friends I've had and I feel a connection.

The two men finally pause a moment and glance in my direction. One offers a smile and a wave. My movie plans forgotten for a moment, I'm drawn to these fascinating little planes and their unusual operators. I casually approach, not sure how to initiate the conversation. "Hello there." I call out. "Excuse me. I was just driving by, and stopped because I was curious about your planes. I was wondering if you need some kind of license to fly these planes."

The taller one, who appears to be about fifty, smartly replies, "Yeah, a, uh, PILOT'S license."

Okay, I guess that was a dumb question. But I feel like I need to establish a dialogue with these two guys to find out more. I try another question, "Your planes sure look fun. What are you guys up to out here?"

The pilot of the green plane, Rich, who looks about 35 years old, is now gathering small green melons from the side of the dirt road, and loading them into the right seat of his plane. He pauses to reply, "We're flying reconnaissance sorties, performing intelligence gathering, and striking enemy positions to re-establish total air superiority."

Dan chuckles good-naturedly. "Yeah, and God knows Rich could REALLY use a lot more intelligence gathering! What he means is that we're just buzzing around dropping these wild watermelons on an old sunken boat out on the river for fun. We don't mean any harm because we just do it for the challenge."

On the verge of another dumb question I ask, "Aren't these planes dangerous to fly?"

As those words left my mouth I hoped they wouldn't take it the wrong way. I was afraid the question I just posed might imply they were either stupid or insane for flying their little planes.

Rich's face becomes serious and he answers, "Maybe. But I think my life is at a greater risk if I DON'T fly them!"

That was indeed a strange answer. How could it be more dangerous to stay on the ground? I try a few more questions, "What are they? How high and fast can they go? What's the horsepower? Where do you keep them?"

I could see the two men become bored with my questions, but Dan politely answers anyway. "They're two seat ultralights, but the FAA has recently categorized them as sport planes because technically ultralights are only supposed to have a single seat. These planes takeoff at about twenty miles per hour, and in cruise they go about fifty. They can get as high as 20,000 feet, but the real fun is down low. We run a two cycle engine which puts out sixty five horsepower, and we keep them in a hangar not too far from here at a private airstrip."

Their planes look simple in design, but sophisticated enough to be high performance versatile machines. With open cockpits, and exposed to nature's elements it must be an intimate way to experience flight; low and slow taking in the scenery. I can think of several other questions, but I don't want to keep them any longer. As I start back to my truck I offer a wave and shout, "Hey thanks for the info. I'll let you get back to your bombing missions! See you around."

With their munitions of wild watermelons they mount up and promptly prepare for flight. Fascinated, I stand in front of my truck to watch. Seatbelts fastened and headsets on, they yell, "Clear!" With a yank on the starter handle their engines purr to life letting off a wisp of blue smoke.

With a burst of power and cloud of dust they lift off in a surprisingly short distance. Leveling at ten feet high, the two small craft skim slowly over the tops of the cornfields in tight formation. Appearing to be joined at the wings they slowly shrink into the distance.

Isn't it every child's dream to fly like a bird? Open-mouthed and in awe, I am left alone to imagine their adventures and certain amusement.

For a moment I dare to wonder what it would be like to go for a ride, but quickly dismiss the thought; I can't even stand to fly in a big jetliner let alone an ultralight. The notion of being up over the fields and looking down at the earth below with nothing but thin air between, sends a tingling sensation from my stomach up my spine and into the

Chapter 3
Possessed

I'm not sure we're going to make it in time. Narrow two lane country roads aren't the safest of places. I push it up a little over the speed limit, but there's no sense in risking my family's lives just to see a movie. I hate being rushed. Sometimes I think I need to plan my time better, but then I hadn't expected to be distracted earlier.

Sure enough when we arrive at the mall we are too late for the five o'clock show. Jennifer and Shannon aren't too disappointed though because there's always shopping to be had. The three of us venture out to check out the mall. The girls gravitate toward clothing stores, and I find myself in search of a sporting goods shop.

Fortunately the mall isn't busy for a Saturday. Lately, when I'm in crowds I get edgy. It's not as bad as the reaction I get on a jetliner, but I feel vulnerable to panic attacks. I'm not sure what it is, but I start to feel anxious and trapped. This is a fairly new problem for me, so I haven't had a chance to discuss it with anyone yet. I seem to be battling some nagging anxiety in my life that is compounded by crowded situations.

Walking back toward our meeting place, I'm not surprised to see that Jennifer has bought new school clothes for Shannon and both of them beam satisfied smiles at me as they approach. With a good appetite worked up, we decide to get dinner at a Mexican restaurant.

As we sit down and check the menu, Shannon turns to her Mom. "I bet Dad will get the 'usual' - again!" The thing about American style Mexican food is that it is made up of mostly the same stuff just packaged differently. Wrap it in a tortilla and it's a burrito. Place it in a "U" shape and it's a taco. Place it on its side and it's a quesadilla. As the girls know, I like to order the chimichunga, not for the taste, but just because it's fun to say.

I love spending time with my family. Shannon is a senior in high school and will soon be off at college. She's a very bright kid, and as an only child she acts quite mature for her age. I don't know what happened to the time. It seems cliché but it feels like it was just yesterday she was daddy's little girl learning to ride a bike.

The three of us talk over the options for Shannon's college education over pre-meal chips and salsa. I'm surprised to find I'm lobbying for her to attend a college within driving distance of home. Am I being selfish because I never want to set foot on an airplane again? The thought of having to fly to visit my daughter is almost enough to ruin my appetite.

After discussing a variety of issues I bring up the reason why I was late this afternoon. I describe the strange little airplanes and the two characters I met earlier. As the girls listen to my account I can tell they sense my excitement and intrigue. I'm astonished that machines exist that allow people to roam as they please, not held captive by ordinary boundaries like fences or gravity. Anyone can be free as a bird if they want!

With her eyes wide, sweet Shannon says, "Dad that sounds so cool! They were just flying around the cornfields by our house? How come I've never seen them? Do you think they're safe? Are you going to learn to fly?"

Smiling, Jennifer asks, "Mark, haven't you always had an interest in flying? I remember you and your dad always talking about planes, but I had the feeling lately you weren't so keen on airline travel. Doesn't flying bother you?"

I am somewhat surprised by Jennifer's question. I've never mentioned my fears to her and once again I think how unfair it is that women have an intuition that allows them to see right through you like Superman's x-ray vision.

Sometimes it's hard to get a word in with these two

girls, and before I can respond, Shannon speaks up again. "Dad, I didn't know you hated flying. You know my friend Cindy's mom hates flying too. She even gets sick at the thought of getting on an airliner. Cindy says her mom is really embarrassed by it too."

Finally a break in the conversation allows me to jump in. "You know I have to admit that lately flying has really bothered me. I had a real hard time on that trip to my class reunion."

Jennifer lays her hand over mine and replies, "Honey, a lot of people have trouble with flying. When I fly I just grin and bear it because I have no idea how those big planes can get up off the ground. I just try to trust that the crew knows what they're doing, and they've done it before. Mark, maybe if you learned more about the little planes, and learned about the basics of flight, it would help you feel better."

"Yeah, I'm sorry I've never said anything about it before. Still, those little planes looked like so much fun. I've always toyed with the idea of learning to fly, but I'm not sure if I can now. Maybe I'm getting too old. Besides, I'm not sure this is the way to go about getting over my phobia."

"Mark, you should check into it." Jennifer encourages. "Just make sure it's safe. I think you'd have fun, and Shannon and I would happily volunteer to be your copilot whenever you need one. Remember that time I went parasailing in Mexico? I loved that!"

Shannon chimes in, "Yeah Dad! Maybe I could learn to fly some day too. Hey, aren't you the one who's always saying we shouldn't run away from our nightmares, but run toward our dreams?"

How can she be so wise for a 17 year old kid? I guess after a while some of the advice a parent repeats sinks in after all. "Well, I'll check into it. I'm not going to do anything stupid. If they're not safe then forget it."

*　　*　　*

In the weeks that follow I become a human sponge, a man possessed. Before I know it, I find that every spare minute of the day I look for information on sport flying. I am clearly distracted by this impulse. I investigate the internet, books, and magazines to get a fix for my new obsession on flying. Passions don't come along often in life, so one shouldn't be too quick to dismiss their potential gifts. With that in mind, I continue my research.

For a little perspective I read up on the world's first ultralight, the 1903 Wright Flyer. It was Orville's flight that was the first time a machine carrying a man, and driven by a motor had lifted itself off the ground. The flight lasted twelve seconds, climbed to ten feet, and covered a distance of about 120 feet. The 1903 Flyer weighed slightly more than modern day ultralights at 600 pounds, but it really lacked horsepower. The 1903 Flyer only had twelve horsepower compared to the sixty five commonly used today.

My office staff is very tolerant of my new fixation. Seeing the literature strewn around my office they realize this new project is more than just a passing interest. They tease me good naturedly about having to move the stacks of airplane magazines just to find my in-basket. "Mark, you have so much going for you. Why would you want to risk everything to mess around with ultralights?"

Maybe they're right. Maybe this idea is crazy. One thought keeps bugging me though. That one ultralight pilot, Rich, what did he mean when he said, "I think my life is at greater risk if I don't fly?" And why do I feel like I understand that statement?

Unfortunately ultralights inherited a bad reputation during their infancy. In the beginning several people hurt or killed themselves. The little planes were assembled in garages and in back yards without supervision. People figured they were easy to fly, so as a result many crashed. Ultralights look simple enough, but operating them without adequate guidance or training is dangerous. The ultralight industry now stresses the importance of good construction, maintenance, and getting the proper flight and ground instruction.

Because safety is a huge concern, I scour the literature about ultralight accidents. I learn from everything I read that the majority of accidents are caused by operator error. Common terms used to describe the mishaps include: Failure to maintain flying speed, inadequate preflight inspection, improper maintenance, contaminated fuel or fuel starvation.

I am unable to find many accidents in recent years that are blamed on the ultralight itself. By all accounts these vehicles have evolved into safe machines if utilized properly. Clearly education and proper instruction are essential. I continue my research intensely over the course of the next few weeks. The more I read the more it becomes apparent that the pilot controls his own fate. Ultralights don't kill people; people kill themselves by being careless or reckless.

My personality is a little bit obsessive-compulsive. I enjoy a challenge, and then become obsessed with mastering it. Occasionally taking time off from work to pursue my new interest I drive out near the cornfields hoping to run into Dan and Rich again. I also make a couple of trips out to the local airport, but without luck. There is no way I can break into this sport on my own. Despite all of my preparation, research, and efforts, I would still need help.

Chapter 4
Dreamland

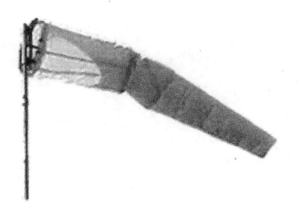

*I*t's a bright, crisp afternoon. My spirits have lifted along with the usual November overcast. I have a feeling my luck will change today too. Leisurely driving amongst the skeletons of dead cornfields in a daydream of flight, I begin to wonder if I'll ever run into Dan or Rich again. I figure on a day like today they'll be out in their planes enjoying the pleasant weather.

It doesn't take long before I spot a familiar looking blue plane flying from left to right not too far out in front of my truck. I zigzag through the fields managing to follow its track. Ignoring the "No Trespassing" and "Keep Out" signs posted along the way, my chase leads me down a private gravel road back to a quaint farm. By the time I find where the plane has landed its engine is already shut off. I recognize the tall pilot, it is Dan. Bundled in a bulky flight suit, wearing gloves, and a scarf draped around his neck, he's just getting up out of the cockpit of his plane.

Gazing around the farm I'm stunned by the surroundings. I've entered a different world, an era lost in time. With my truck engine silent the setting has an eerie quality to it. Bordering the property is a weathered wooden fence. To the west of a lush green runway is a line of Willow trees which delicately sway in the easy breeze. Far to the east are the snow capped Sierra-Nevada Mountains. Stationed next to the landing strip on top of a large white hangar is a faded orange windsock that hunts endlessly for the wind's origin.

I raise a hand in greeting as I climb out of my truck and venture over to have a better look at Dan's plane. I quickly appreciate the meticulous care evident in its construction. This plane is not just a toy; it's simple, light-

31

weight design appears sturdy and reliable.

Dan must take great pride in his fine flying machine. With all of the research I have done on ultralights, I'm eager to finally get a chance to talk to one of these guys again. Walking toward Dan I say, "Hi there, if you have a minute do you mind if I ask you about your plane?"

Eyeing me with skepticism Dan replies, "No I don't mind, but how did you find this place? We don't have many people wandering back here."

"Do you remember that day you and your buddy were dropping watermelons? Well I was the guy who stopped to watch you. I was impressed with your planes, and was really hoping to find you guys to ask some more questions. By the way my name is Mark, Mark Thomas."

Unlocking the huge door to the hangar he replies, "Well nice to meet you Mark. I'm Daniel Martin. You can call me Dan."

Mounted above the door is an odd looking homemade sign. In large letters it reads; "AREA 52 - TOP SECRET MILITARY INSTALLATION". Below in smaller font reads; "Welcome to Dreamland!"

The real Dreamland is known as Area 51, a top-secret military base located north of Las Vegas. The Air Force controls the base, and it's known for testing exotic aircraft, and is rumored to house UFO's. Shaking my head a little, I mutter, "Who are these guys and what the heck am I getting myself into?"

Inside the hangar I can see Rich's green plane way in the back. The place is clean and well lit. It has workbenches, shelves stocked with airplane parts, a refrigerator, some comfy chairs, and even a nice stereo system. This hangar looks like a comfortable place to spend some time.

Dan is extremely helpful and patient with all of my questions. We discuss many aspects of sport flying including methods for assembling the plane and flying lessons. As he carefully pushes his plane into the hangar I tell him,

"You know I've read up a lot on your model of ultralight, and it appears to have the best safety record in the industry. I'm thinking about ordering a kit for a plane just like yours."

Surprised, Dan studies me with interest. "Huh. No kidding? Sometimes when Rich and I are out flying we get people interested in our planes. But few ever follow up on their dreams of flight because the sport requires such large commitment; which," he pauses to look directly at me, "if you're serious, you'll soon discover for yourself."

Assembling a new plane would require a space bigger than my garage because the plane's wing span is over 30 feet. Although I've been anxious to get started on my own plane, I haven't been able to find the space to accommodate my project. I tell Dan, "I've been out to the local general aviation airport, but there are no hangars available."

"Yeah, you sure you want to do this?" He asks.

I tell him of my obsession over the last few months; countless hours scouring the internet, book stores and aviation magazines. Apparently impressed with my tenacity, Dan offers, "If you're that committed, I can invite you to join us in our hangar. We have room for one more plane, and you can help pay the rent on the building. I'll even help you with some of the more difficult portions of the assembly."

This generosity is more than I expected or even hoped for. Excited by this new prospect and wanting to know more, I ask, "Do you and Rich own this property?"

Wiping the exhaust residue from the propeller with an old rag, Dan informs me, "No, the property is owned by a special old gal who's an aviation fanatic from way back. She used to be quite a pilot years ago, but she's no longer able to fly. She likes watching our small planes buzzing around though, and occasionally we take her along for a flight. She spends most of her time reading and attending to her tropical pet birds."

Motioning to the other end of the runway, Dan continues, "That's her house over there. Every once in a while she'll come over and join in on the hangar flying. Her name's Amelia and this private airstrip is known to the small society of ultralight pilots in the area as Dreamland. Rich and I pay a modest rent, and help out around the property taking care of Amelia's place and keeping up the grass runway."

The luscious grass landing strip is manicured like a golf course, and from a short distance it looks like an inviting soft sea of green. Dreamland is indeed a good description for the place. It's an ideal setting for a private airstrip. And like the fabled Area 51 Dreamland in the Nevada desert, this place too has strange vehicles, and secret operations conducted far from public view.

*   *   *

That night at home I describe Dreamland to Jennifer and Shannon. Excitedly, I tell them everything Dan said. I may be a little too in touch with my inner child, but I can no longer help myself. After dinner Shannon retreats to her room to catch up on the day's gossip with her girlfriends on the phone. Taking advantage of the privacy, I explain to Jennifer the plan I've been formulating. "You know I've been reading a lot about flying. Maybe I'm being a little impulsive, but I think I'm ready to order a kit for a plane. According to Dan it's pretty easy to assemble. It only takes a few weeks to put together, and he said he'd help me with the hard parts. When I'm done, he says he can teach me how to fly, too."

I couldn't ask for a more understanding mate than Jennifer. Over the years she has put up with my obsessions and encouraged me even when she had her doubts about my endeavors. Now, true to her character, she smiles and calmly responds, "Mark you know I support you on this.

I've seen how careful you are with everything else you've ever done. I know you're prepared. If this is what you want, then I think you should go ahead and pursue it."

"I've given it a lot of thought, you know. I've weighed the pros and cons and I just can't get it out of my mind." Laughing, I remind her of the time she insisted on redecorating our kitchen. She spent weeks puzzling over tile and countertops, faucets and cabinet faces. She forced me to look at countless paint and wallpaper samples and generally became a pest to Shannon and me before she was finally satisfied with a design. Promising to spare her that kind of badgering I ask, "So you don't mind if I order it tomorrow? It's really not too expensive."

Jennifer wisecracks, "Okay, but as long as I get to pick out a nice big diamond ring." Giving me a warm smile and a hug, she says, "Just kidding, honey! Go order your airplane."

The next day at the office I make the call to the manufacturer. My hands shake while I give my credit card number and shipping information. Everyone in the office thinks I'm nuts, but what's new!

That night I could hardly sleep thinking about how my life will change. I'll be busy with this new endeavor, but if I schedule my time wisely I shouldn't have to sacrifice too much time away from my family. Since the clinic has been making good money lately, I rationalize that I can also reduce my workload a little.

Two weeks later Christmas arrives early for me. Instead of colorfully wrapped presents delivered by sleigh, my packages are large plain cardboard boxes brought by a big brown truck. I am no less excited by their arrival than a six year old on Christmas morning. I sit there for a while, and stare at those boxes to consider the magic they surely hold.

*   *   *

The very next weekend I haul the boxes containing my new airplane parts out to the hangar. Dan is already there at Dreamland tinkering on his plane's engine. Rich's plane is gone, and Dan shows me which part of the hangar to unload at and claim as my own. An old woman drives up in a red Volkswagen Bug and I wonder if this could be our landlord with the rental agreements for me to sign.

The woman is dressed in a tropical flowered blouse and baggy beige slacks. She gets out of the car, and walks slowly and carefully over to the hangar's entrance. She is fairly tall, and probably in her eighties or early nineties. She has a weathered, familiar looking face with a faint scar on her forehead. She has many wrinkles, but somehow they work for her. She is tan, trim, and healthy looking. Envisioning her as a younger woman, I figure she probably had her share of attention from men in her day.

"Hey Dan, is this your new hangar-mate?" The woman calls out.

Dan walks out and greets her with a big friendly hug, "Hey Amelia, how are you doing? Yeah this here's Mark. I told you about him. He's new to sport flying, and he just got a new kit to build."

Amelia has a demure smile and her eyes squint from the light of the sun. She lowers her hand from shading her face, and cordially offers it to me, "Nice to have you aboard. My name's Amelia."

Her hand is soft yet firm in mine. As she releases our clasp I say, "Nice to meet you Amelia. I feel darned lucky to have found this place, and Dan is making me feel at home here."

"Good to hear. You can work out the rent payments with Dan and Rich. All I ask is that when you get ready to fly you just don't buzz too low over my neighbors. I hope you enjoy yourself, and just be careful. Other than that, maybe offer me a ride once in a while," she says with a wink.

I instantly feel welcome here. Dan is generous, and Amelia has a unique motherly charisma about her. She mentions something about feeding her birds, and then slowly motors off in her Bug.

"That's a great landlord you got there." I say to Dan.

Laughing, he says, "You mean that's a great land-lord WE'VE got!"

"Hey Dan, I couldn't help notice the scar on Amelia's forehead. Did she get that flying? And it's none of my business, but what kind of flying did she do anyway?"

Dan considers this for a moment then says, "Well Mark, all she's told me was that she used to fly all over the place, and that she got the scar in a little mishap while flying a long time ago. She says she's a widow, and that her husband left her enough money to live on this farm far away from nosey people. She likes the peace and quiet out here - except of course for our planes. I think she wishes she had one herself!"

I know from my Dad's history lessons that Amelia Earhart attempted a daring round-the-world flight long ago. She left Oakland, California back in 1937 in a big aluminum twin engine tail dragger. Her course took her east to Florida across the Atlantic over Africa, Asia, Australia, and over the Pacific. But she vanished somewhere near Howland Island in the South Pacific never to be heard from again.

I wished my father were here. I bet he would have some questions to ask. And now that Dan piqued my interest I can't avoid inquiring, "Let me get this straight. Amelia is an old gal with a mysterious past who used to be a pilot? C'mon Dan! What's the real story here?"

Again Dan takes his time responding, and with a wry smile adds, "You believe what you want Mark. Rich has his own theory, but mind you, Rich is a little out there. I think he even believes in UFO's and stuff. Anyway, he thinks Amelia is the real deal. He says she got her scar from crashing her plane at Howland Island during her round-the-world attempt. Rich swears he read somewhere that Howard Hughes, also an accomplished pilot, organized a secret search and recovery mission to find Miss Earhart. He believes Hughes did indeed find her living on the island, and he brought her back. Rich thinks they secretly got married, and that when Hughes died she bought this farm, and has lived out here ever since."

In a disbelieving tone I say, "No way! You guys are full of it!"

Dan replies, "You probably got that right! Listen we have a good set up here. We have a great place to keep our planes, and Amelia is about the best landlord you could ask for. I have never pushed her much about her past. She's kind of reluctant to talk too much about it, but I'm okay with it. Heck she's probably just a senile old lady living in her own fantasy world. That's fine by me!"

Trying to settle down a bit I remark, "All right Dan, I'll let it go. She is real friendly, and I can tell she's the type who enjoys airplanes, and takes a lot of pride in her little piece of heaven here."

As I get back to unloading my boxes the hangar's stereo plays old hits from the Big Band era on a scratchy AM station. We hear songs from Glenn Miller, Benny Goodman, Duke Ellington, and Louis Armstrong. When I question him, Dan says the radio reception is poor inside the hangar, and ironically that's the only station they can get.

Laying flat on the hangar floor next to Dan and his plane is an old German Shepherd. It lies quietly never moving from the spot. After Dan helps unload my boxes I kneel down to say hello to his dog, "What's your dog's name?"

"His name's Jetlag. I adopted him from a shelter about five years ago, and he's never been what I would call real spunky."

After examining the dog's teeth, eyes, and hips I can see that Jetlag has a congenital disease common among German Shepherds. "You know I'm a veterinarian, and I see a lot of this breed with arthritis in their rear hip joints. I'll bring out some Rimadyl arthritis medicine for him. You should also consider feeding him dog food containing Glucosamine because it's helped a lot of other dogs with their painful joints."

"Ritalin? How much will that cost?" Dan asks as he grabs a feeler gauge to check his engine's spark plug gap.

"No, Rimadyl! And it's no charge, my pleasure. By the way, what do you do for work?"

"I'm an airline mechanic out at San Francisco Airport. Normally I help rebuild Pratt and Whitney turbine engines. I've been out there for about twenty four years. I used to do line maintenance; you know when a plane breaks down at the gate? But there are too many people asking questions about how soon the plane will be fixed. That gets annoying, so I like the engine shop now because it's a little more relaxed."

I begin to cut open my cardboard boxes trying not to look too much like a kid ripping open his presents, "Airline mechanic, huh? I don't know why, and I've never really admitted this to anyone, but I hate riding in the back of those big planes. Last time I flew I nearly freaked out. I just can't believe something so huge can fly - let alone stay together in turbulence. And I wonder how much the airlines are cutting costs these days?"

Dan finishes replacing his spark plugs, and wipes his hands with a rag, "You know I've heard a lot of people have a fear of flying. More than most of us realize. I think it's like one in six! I guess with some people it's a control issue. Trusting your life to someone you've never met is tough. I've known a number of airline pilots, and they're really the cream of the crop. The airlines are able to attract the best pilots because the job is so rewarding."

I stop opening boxes to listen better, and ask, "So they're well qualified? You wouldn't worry about the skill level or training of the pilots?"

Dan replies, "Those guys go through so much training, retraining, and check rides that they stay really sharp. Every six months they've got to go through a tough medical exam too. They're human, but those guys know what there doing!"

Though he eases my fear about the pilots a little, I bring up another concern, "So explain how something that big gets off the ground and manages to stay together in bad turbulence."

Dan's confidence in this subject matter is contagious. I'm grateful he is taking the time to share some of his knowledge and we pass the time amicably. For the most part I simply soak in all he has to say.

"Big airplanes fly the same as small ones. Basically, wings and some speed through the air is all that is required to make a plane fly. The plane is just moving through the air like swimming or surfing. Air is like water, a fluid. It's just a little thinner than water, but it is still a significant mass. Have you ever stuck your hand out the car window on the freeway? The faster you go the thicker the air feels, right? To a plane, traveling over 500 mph, it feels like a thick fluid capable of substantial support. Jetliners look massive, but for their size they are lightweight. For the most part they are hollow, constructed primarily with lightweight aluminum. Just think of a soda can."

Moving around his plane to check the adjustment of his hand brake, Dan goes on. "As for the plane's strength, the FAA mandates that jetliners are designed and built with large safety margins. Coming out of the factory the planes are thoroughly flight tested before certification. Structurally, jet aircraft can withstand many times the stresses and forces which are imposed upon them in normal flight profiles."

Jetlag's face contorts as Dan reaches down to scratch behind the dogs ears. "The wing of an aircraft is incredibly strong. It's built as one continuous unit extending through the fuselage. It's constructed with huge reinforced spars. Unless they are flown at speeds far greater than normal, there is no way the wing of an aircraft can produce enough lift to damage its structure. This also applies to turbulence because even severe turbulence won't harm an aircraft. The wings just can't produce enough of a lifting force to bend anything."

With furrowed eyebrows I say, "That's what really bugs me, turbulence."

"People often misunderstand turbulence. When encountering turbulence, nervous passengers feel that the plane is falling out of the sky. It's natural for them to only feel the down bumps. But actually, for every down bump there is an up bump. The down bumps are just more easily noticed. Turbulence bad enough to spill drinks or cause you to fly up off your seat is extremely rare. But even if you do experience it, remember that the plane is not falling thousands of feet. It just hit a bump a couple of feet high. The altimeters in the cockpit would barely register the bump. According to the National Transportation Safety Board there has never been a modern airliner that crashed because of turbulence alone. Turbulence may be annoying, even unnerving, but it can't make the wings break."

Then I ask, "But what about air pockets? Can't they be dangerous if a plane falls into one?"

Dan takes a deep breath, grins and sighs, "I don't know where the whole air pocket fabrication started, but there are no such things as air pockets! You can think of flying like being on a lake in a boat. Sometimes the lake waters are smooth, and sometimes they get stirred up from the wind or other planes. Riding on a choppy lake may be a bumpy ride. Sometimes you might encounter a big wave that jolts the boat. Riding the down side of a wave may give you the feeling you're dropping. But there are no holes or pockets in the water where the boat, or plane, is going to fall into. Air pockets are a myth because planes don't just fall out of the sky. There is always air there to support them!"

"Man!" I declare, "I wish I would have known some of that stuff before. I think you're starting to put me more at ease about flying on those big planes."

Dan smartly replies, "Hey, it's no charge, Doc!"

From the distance the sound of a two stroke engine becomes distinct. We look outside the hangar to see the bright blue sky has now morphed to a darker violet color as the sun has ducked behind the hills to the west. The silhouette of Rich's ultralight is apparent just above the horizon to the south. Descending to the runway, Rich eases the throttle back and his little plane's wheels softly kiss the welcoming grass carpet. He pulls up to the hangar with his propeller coasting to a stop.

Rich is not alone. In the right seat dressed in a cute pink snow suit is a little toe-headed blonde girl. She must be his daughter, and her ear to ear grin strains the limits of her facial muscles. Exiting the plane they giggle to one another and tell of their adventure finding a hidden cave up in the foothills. His daughter is clutching interesting rocks and other artifacts found there. I don't know if I have ever witnessed a stronger display of love and connection than that which passed between this father and daughter.

Now that I get the chance to formally meet Richard Hansen I find out he is a vice president at a big telecommunications company. With all the seriousness of his business world he likes to come out here to blow off a little steam with some, as Rich puts it, aeronautical silliness.

While Dan and I help Rich put his plane to bed, I learn that Rich grew up in Montana, and graduated from UC Berkeley. Rich never stops. He's a funny guy who is always quick with a joke. Rich could easily afford other aircraft, but says he prefers his little ultralight to any other plane he could think of. He loves the intimacy of low and slow flying, and says it's the closest you can come to flying like a bird without going through the whole re-incarnation thing!

Chapter 5
Building Trust

Long fluorescent lights hang from the high ceiling, and an old, but clean carpet blankets the concrete floor. A portable propane heater hisses to warm the chilly winter air which snakes its way inside our hangar. Jetlag lies on his side not far from the warmth of the glowing heat.

The kit was shipped from the factory in large boxes containing cardboard sheets. Each sheet holds shrink-wrapped parts which are labeled with an identifying number. Dan helps me to take inventory of my new kit. He's told me this is an important step. Dan has assembled many of these planes before, and if I am missing any parts it is best to let the factory know now, so obtaining correct parts won't hold up the assembly process.

Rich is often busy with family life, and sometimes his work will overflow into the weekends. It is good to see him out at the hangar today. He was really hoping to fly, but the weather isn't so great. Always full of energy, Rich hangs a new aviation calendar above the workbench. Twelve glossy pages of beefcake beauties posed alongside famous World War II planes.

With that task complete, Rich looks for something else he's qualified to undertake. He may know his way around a printed circuit board, but according to Dan, nuts and bolts must beware of his presence. Dan often gets nervous when Rich handles tools around airplanes. Rich is a natural born seat-of-the-pants pilot with an adventurous spirit, but Dan has always helped him when it came to doing any maintenance on Rich's plane. Most of the time Dan volunteers to work on Rich's plane rather than watch Rich screw it up, only to have Dan fix it anyway.

The assembly manual for my kit is well written, and

each instruction is clearly stated. Rich, unsuccessfully finding any new projects, hovers overhead while munching on some potato chips. Dan helps me to get started with step one: "Attach item A to item B securing with bolt C and nut D".

Taking my time and care with the straight forward process I make casual conversation, "So how did you guys get into sport flying?"

Rich responds, "About four years ago I was water-skiing with my buddies out in the Delta when I met Dan flying around on floats. I thought it was the coolest thing how he could buzz around overhead, and splash down wherever he wanted. So anyway, Dan helped me get started in the sport too. Since then I've tried flying larger airplanes. They're great for getting you to your destination, but sometimes I think it's not so important where you go, but how you get there!"

As I assemble the first pieces of my kit, Dan shows me how to torque the nut so as not to distort the aluminum tubing. He warns me not to allow the bolt to spin while tightening, because that can score the shank of the bolt, and leave it weakened. "How about you Dan, how did you get started?"

"I used to hang glide back in the early eighties. For a lot of us it just naturally evolved into ultralighting, and then from there to sport flying. I was an instructor for a while on the side, but it's difficult to make much money, so now I just like to fly for fun."

Rich, quickly bored, heads over to his plane to put a little more air into his under inflated tires. Dan watches Rich, and doesn't seem to consider this to be too much of a threat to Rich's plane.

Privately I ask Dan, "Do you ever feel afraid when you're up there?"

"Well I might get a little nervous sometimes. But if I'm getting too nervous, that tells me I must be doing something wrong. See, when flying, you want to stay mentally ahead of your airplane. You have to plan and visualize what's coming up next. That way if you don't like what is going to happen next, you will have the time to change your course of action. So if I begin to feel too nervous, it's time to change what I'm doing. Slow the plane down, climb to a higher and safer altitude, turn back, stop for more fuel, etc. The fun thing about flying is that you are in control, or at least you should be! If you don't like a particular situation you can change it. A good pilot never gets boxed into a position where there isn't a comfortable way to get out. You know, keep your options open. Good pilots try hard not to scare themselves."

Dan holds onto a bracket for me while I struggle to insert a metal rod into a closely fitted slot. "But how do you know when each and every situation is safe?" I ask.

"In aviation there is no such thing as something being *maybe* safe. If you think a situation is *maybe* safe, then you must consider it to be *unsafe*. All *maybes* fall into the *no* category. You must be absolutely sure it is safe, or you don't do it."

Nodding, I respond, "Sounds kind of black and white."

"Yep."

*   *   *

The cage structure of the cockpit has been completed on my first weekend of assembly. I am happy with the results, and appreciate all I've learned hangar flying on this rainy Sunday afternoon.

The very next weekend Dan and Rich are unable to come out, but I manage to get the tail section started on my own. It is on this day that Amelia graces me with her presence. As it isn't too cold out, she comes by to keep me company.

My first impression of her was that she was shy, but now I see her opening up more. I know not to breach the subject of Amelia's past by how she always turns the conversation to the present. I find her a fantastic resource of information and wisdom. I'm surprised at how quickly I feel at ease discussing some of my concerns. While I work on my plane's rudder our friendship grows, and I begin to confide in her. I explain my increasing phobia about airline travel, and the uncertainly I have over whether I might ever learn how to fly this plane I am building.

At a good stopping point I put down the rudder and turn to her. "I hate this fear of flying I have. It's affected my life in more ways than I would have ever imagined. I'm ashamed to admit my fears, but I've got to do something. I miss out on vacations, business conferences, and it spills over into other areas of my life. How can I allow this fear to control my life this way?"

Sitting in a chair near the workbench, Amelia replies, "I think if you were to look at what motivates us, you would find fear plays an important role. In our world fear is common. We fear change; we fear stagnation. We fear dying; we fear living. We fear crowds; we fear loneliness. Fear affects our lives in so many ways. I don't know that fear is so much a psychological problem as an educational issue. Fear is the result of how we perceive a threat or a danger. If we could learn more about unfamiliar situations, and become convinced that we could handle them, the fear would naturally subside."

Sitting down in a chair next to Amelia with my elbows on my knees I say, "But I detest my fear. It's gotten so bad that now when I'm on a jetliner I'm afraid I'm just going to go crazy. It's like I'm afraid of panicking, and then I worry that my racing heart will cause a coronary or I might just pass out!"

Amelia considers for a moment. "Mark, I know it's hard to believe, but fear is actually a good thing. Fear acts as one of our defense mechanisms. It prepares us to fight or flee. It is an important emotion that protects us. The thing to remember when you feel these reactions and symptoms is that they may feel uncomfortable, but they won't physically hurt you. You won't lose control, faint, or have a heart attack. You're experiencing a healthy fear reaction just as nature intended."

"And another thing," as she places a hand on my leg, "often people who have strong fears also possess an overactive imagination. For example, they might hear an unfamiliar noise during a flight, and begin imagining what might be wrong with the plane. Or, they may believe in signs or have premonitions their plane will crash. They might have a dream or hear a song about an accident. Sometimes books or movies use dreams to give the story a supernatural or surreal feel. Those may be entertaining, but you should try to stick with reality and facts. A lot of people subconsciously believe they have ESP, but odds are they are not psychic!"

Remembering how I'd reacted to the "American Pie" song on my flight to Denver I feel a sinking sensation in my stomach. She was right! How could some stupid lyrics in a song affect my flight? She seems to know exactly how to address my concerns.

Standing up, heading for the refrigerator I say, "You know, I feel better just talking about it. Would you care for a cola?"

Amelia slowly rises and accepts my offer. After a few sips I decide it's time to get back to work. I start on the difficult task of finishing the tail's horizontal stabilizer. This is the part of the tail that the elevator is hinged to. Earlier, I put off this segment of the assembly because I knew it wouldn't be easy.

Sure enough, while trying to get the tight fabric pulled over the tail section I get frustrated, and find myself swearing at the seemingly impossible task. In my bafflement I complain, "I don't know if this is worth it. What am I doing? Sometimes this damn plane just won't cooperate! Maybe I should give up on this idea of flying anyway!"

Amelia absently runs her hand along the wing of Dan's plane and continues, "Mark, you don't yet appreciate the magic you hold in your hands. You are so close to a miracle you don't realize it. Throughout man's long history people have dreamt of the marvel of flight. It has only been in the brief era of the last generation that this has been possible. With a scant few nuts and bolts you possess the powers the ancient Greeks like Icarus coveted. Relax Mark. You will soon be flying high in the sky, close to the sun, without the concerns of melting wings!"

With that, Amelia eases away from Dan's plane, and explains she must head back home leaving me to put away my tools, and close up the hangar. I haven't given up on the tail yet, I'll just need some help.

*   *   *

The next weekend Dan makes it out and Amelia comes by too. This time she has one of her exotic birds with her. It is an African Grey parrot named Howie. African Grey's are one of the most intelligent and best speaking birds among the parrot species. Many show a definite preference for only one human. All African Grey parrots have the potential to speak and imitate not only human, but all types of sounds. As I would find out, this particular bird is a little bit of a trouble maker.

Dan helps me to finish the tail with ease. As we work on assembling the wings, Howie has a little fun with Jetlag. I guess somewhere along the line Howie must have been around a cat, because just as Jetlag starts to doze off, Howie lets out a long, "Meeeooow!"

Hearing this, Jetlag's head pops up off the floor, he looks around, and then bellows an instinctive, "Woof!"

I can hardly believe it, but that damn parrot chuckles, "Ha, ha, ha, ha."

Poor old Jetlag, about the time he relaxes and closes his eyes again Howie starts the process all over with another, "Meeeooow!"

This goes on for most of the day. Amelia, wrapped in a warm sweater, seems satisfied to sit quietly and watch Dan and I work on my project while Howie perches on her shoulder.

My plane's wing resembles the shape of a ladder. There is a leading edge spar and trailing edge spar, with struts and ribs connecting the two. Once the basic structure of each wing is complete, Dan helps me slip on the pre-sewn Dacron fabric covering.

Endlessly impressed with Dan's skill and knowledge, I bring up the subject of airline maintenance, "Dan, how can I trust the people who are responsible for the plane I'm riding on. Of course, I wouldn't mind if YOU were always my mechanic."

"First of all, the FAA helps to insure safety by monitoring and certifying all of the safety related people who work in aviation. Then there's a natural tendency for each worker to not only take pride in their own work, but also to keep an eye on others. Because we understand the importance of our work on the safety of passengers, we won't tolerate anything less than perfection. We put our own families on those airplanes!"

Now that I got him going I thought I would pick his brain a bit more, "They say jet engines are pretty reliable. How do they work?"

With the fabric over the wing, Dan smoothes out the wrinkles with his hands. "Turbine engines are simple. They don't have parts moving in every direction like a piston engine. Jet engines just have a series of spinning turbine fans. Air goes in the front, it is compressed by fans, fuel is introduced and burned, and the high pressure exhaust gases spin more fans to create thrust. Once the fuel starts burning, it keeps burning. Just continue adding fuel and the engine continues running. They're really very straightforward and dependable."

As I do my best to mimic Dan's motions to smooth the fabric from the opposite side of the wing I hear another, "Meeeooow!"

Shortly thereafter is the sound of, "Woof!"

Followed by a predictable, "Ha, ha, ha, ha."

Amelia smirks as if she feels responsible for her bird's behavior and adds, "Howie, shame on you..."

Dan continues, "A lot of people think it is the engines which keep the plane in the air. The engines don't make lift. The engines just provide the push to keep the plane moving forward. And without the engine's push a plane can glide incredibly well by pointing the nose slightly downward. This provides the necessary speed. In fact, jetliners glide on just about every flight to save fuel. Normally, about 100 miles from the airport the pilots will bring the throttles back to idle, and let the plane glide all the way to the airport. Then just before landing the pilots increase the power to prepare for any unexpected events, such as a go around."

With the right wing covered, Dan prepares the left wing for the fabric. "Also Mark, every important system on a jetliner has backups. Redundancy is there not only for safety, but for reliability too. If the jetliner isn't dependable the airline loses money. But really, safety is an airline's most important product. CEO's know that if the customer no longer considers his company's airline safe, the party's over. The shareholders will can him in a New York second!"

These sessions out at the hangar are more valuable to me in getting over my fears than any clinic or course I could attend. In the meantime my plane's almost done. Over the next few weekends Dan and I put the finishing touches on my new plane. He shares a great deal of his expertise during the assembly process, and I must admit I am quite happy with the results. My plane looks great with its glossy red wings and tail.

While building it, I have learned what every little nut, bolt, and cable is for. I feel I'm more thoroughly familiar with this piece of machinery than anything I have worked on before. During our days in the hangar Dan and Amelia have coached me in the ways of flying. I have enjoyed wearing a mechanic's hat, but my next step is to trade it in for a pilot's hat. It looks like I'm about to face my greatest fear head on!

Chapter 6
Testing Limits

*T*he day is finally full of dazzling sun and light winds. The last two weekends were dark and dreary. Dan is busy oiling the hangar doors and performing other chores around the property. He is frequently interrupted by Jetlag, insisting he throw his ball. It's great to see Dan's old dog feeling better.

Tinkering, that's all I'm doing today. I check every electrical connection, every nut, every bolt, and every control hinge attachment. I wipe off all smudges and fingerprints from my plane. I apply Armor All Protectant to the sidewalls of the three tires and to the black leather seat covers. I have done all of this before, now I'm doing it again.

"What are you up to Mark? Are you stalling? Don't you think it's about time we smashed some bugs onto that thing? Here, toss me the keys." Dan suggests as he and Jetlag wander over.

These little planes use ignition switches, not keys. But I know what he means, and I'm excited at the thought of Dan taking my plane up for its maiden test flight. "I was hoping you would take her up. I told Jennifer my caterpillar was probably going to spout its wings and fly today."

"Well Mark; let's see if your new butterfly is airworthy first."

Dan always does a thorough preflight on his own plane and he is in no hurry inspecting mine. One doesn't want any unexpected surprises on a plane's first test flight.

Last weekend Dan helped me perform a ground break-in and adjustment of the engine, so everything is ready to go today. Dan starts the engine with one pull from the starter handle above his head and studies the engine instruments. He buckles in and taxis out to the runway. Performing an engine run up, he checks the controls and makes sure the fuel selector lever is turned on.

Amelia happens by and stands with me and Jetlag to watch Dan take my plane up. Even though Dan and Rich occasionally take Amelia flying, I see by the look in her eyes that she probably doesn't get enough time in the air herself.

Dan runs the engine at idle for what seems like ten minutes while sitting in position on the runway. When we hear the engine finally throttle up, Jetlag offers a "woof" as if to grant his owner takeoff clearance.

The plane darts forward. Upon lift off, I can guarantee that I have more butterflies in my stomach than the always unflappable Dan has probably had in a lifetime. In the cool, thick morning air my plane launches skyward as if it had been awaiting permission to be unleashed from gravity's tight grip. Dan climbs high over Dreamland to circle at a safe altitude while checking out all the controls and engine instruments.

Each of our planes is fitted with ballistic parachutes. With one pull of the emergency handle, a rocket motor would propel the parachute canopy out for quick deployment. The chute is attached by a thick cable to the top of the plane's main spar. After deployment the occupants would have to do nothing but ride slowly back to earth. I read a few old stories of crippled ultralights successfully deploying at altitudes as low as 100 feet. Our model sport plane has a good safety record, but it's nice to have the parachute as a backup.

Fortunately Dan will not need the ballistic parachute today because everything on the plane performs flawlessly. When he finally returns to terra firma, he is obviously pleased with its performance.

Shutting down the engine, Dan sits in my plane with a grin and says, "Hey Mark, you've got one heck of a sweet airplane! But I think I've worked up a bit of an appetite. You want to go get a burger?"

"All right, I'll help you lock up the hangar and we can take my truck. Jetlag can ride in the back and Amelia can go too if she wants."

Amelia glances over at me with a funny look on her face, and her mouth is a bit crooked, "Ah Mark? I think Dan wants to take you to lunch in YOUR PLANE. I don't think he's had enough flying in that new bird of yours yet."

My legs approach spaghetti status and all I can manage to mumble is, "Uh, yeah. Uh, okay. I guess..."

With a sympathetic pat on my back, Amelia leaves me to negotiate with Dan. I knew this moment had to come, but why so soon?

"You know Dan, I'm not sure we should leave Jetlag here all by himself." I plead.

"Good idea. You can hold him in your lap!" Dan shouts sarcastically. "C'mon Mark. Jetlag knows the drill. He'll be fine with Amelia. Now let's get you suited up, you're going to love it!"

After bundling up in my new flight gear, I reluctantly settle into the right seat. Dan is seated next to my left elbow. Our legs stretch out horizontally with our feet each resting comfortably on their respective rudder pedals. The lone control stick is forward and between the seats. All of our planes are designed to be used for student training, so they are set up to be flown from either seat.

Above me is the bright red wing with the engine mounted on top. The black prop swings behind us, and the tail is about six feet farther back. The wing is redundantly secured by eight strong steel cables. Our seats sit low, with our bottoms only inches from the ground. Maybe this won't be too scary, I feel like I'm sitting in a go-kart with wings.

Dan makes sure I'm properly outfitted with warm gloves and flight suit. We wear sunglasses to shield the wind, and headsets so we can communicate. The air temperature is about sixty degrees, so we must protect ourselves from the forty five mile per hour wind chill we will experience while airborne.

As we taxi out to the runway we bump along and I recall my studies of basic airmanship. I watch while Dan does a quick control check: Stick back, tail elevator up. Stick forward, elevator down. This will control the pitch attitude for climbing and descending.

Stick right and left, wing ailerons up and down. The ailerons are used to create differential lift to bank the airplane when we turn.

When the rudder pedals are pushed left and right, the tail's rudder deflects in agreement. This will make the plane yaw left and right.

With the engine instruments up to proper temperature, Dan asks if I'm ready. Quite sure that I am NOT ready, I give him a tentative smile and a thumbs up anyway. Lined up on Dreamland's smooth green runway, I'm astonished by the snappy acceleration as Dan advances the throttle. In a flash the grass is a green blur. In what must only be fifty feet, Dan pulls back a little on the stick, the nose wheel raises, and we leap off the ground.

I find myself suddenly operating on sensory overload: the onslaught of cool air and the snarl of the propeller. Mother Earth, which I happen to be very fond of, falls briskly beneath. All that Dan hears in his headphones is my involuntary chant of, "Oh my God, oh my God."

In a matter of seconds I feel small and naked with nothing under us but thin air and a most solid ground below. My legs are paralyzed, my breathing is furious, and my grip is fast. Glancing sideways I see Dan's teeth exposed as he happily smiles. I'm not sure if he is taking pleasure in my obvious terror, or if it is because he loves flying so much. A part of me hopes his teeth end up caked with disgusting bugs for making me do this!

A funny thing happens however. My shock and fear

is quickly transformed to awe at the beauty which lies before me. My hands relax their grip, and my eyes widen. My whole being soaks in the experience. As we climb above 500 feet a distinct pattern of farm fields are revealed. The vista is like nothing I have seen before. I am now a part of the beautiful blue sky. To be up in the air, without restrictions of view, I feel like a bird. This is flying!

Dan looks content and relaxed. The most intelligent and profound statement I can come up with is, "Unbelievable!"

I gain comfort and confidence knowing Dan is in the left seat. He handles the plane in a careful and professional manner: each control movement smooth and precise, always monitoring the instruments and scanning the sky for potential problems.

Suddenly I'm startled by the spectacle of a big Red-Tailed Hawk flying directly in front of us. His keen eyes momentarily glance our way, and then he redirects his attention to the field below. We are so close I could almost lean forward to pluck feathers from his wing. What a magnificent bird!

I have heard of rare instances where large planes might strike a bird and sustain damage to the jet engines, although I understand they have designed the engines to be more bird resistant. To prevent bird strikes, some airports have even implemented programs to scare away flocks of birds by firing pyrotechnics.

Not sure if Dan has spotted the impending collision I warn, "Lookout Dan, don't hit that hawk!"

Dan laughs at my naiveté. "He could just as easily hit us! We're flying at about the same speed, and that hawk wouldn't let me hit him if I tried. This is his territory. He's the REAL boss up here!"

Feeling foolish, I realize this machine actually blends in with nature, rather than plowing through it. Our flight is more exhilarating than I could have imagined. I can hardly wait to tell the girls about this experience when I get home. They will absolutely not believe it.

When Dan senses I have settled down, he offers me the controls. He first tells me to learn the feel of each control response. A little nervous, I clutch the control stick. With a firm grip, I am anxious to show Dan I can be a good pilot with lightning fast reactions. Sensing each aircraft movement I work the controls to quickly counter. I am determined to prevent the plane from slipping out of control. I manipulate the stick with rapid jerking movements. The plane wobbles, rocks, and pitches about, but I manage to prevent us from tipping over. Struggling vigorously, I say, "I'm doing it!" But it sure is harder than I thought it would be.

Dan allows me a minute of battling with the plane before he finally says, "Whoa Mark! Easy there, you're working way too hard. Why don't you just let go of the stick for a while?"

Hardly able to speak because of my intense concentration on the task at hand, I manage to respond, "Huh? Are you sure? Okay, HERE you take it back."

I tentatively release my grasp of the stick, and to my surprise Dan doesn't grab hold of it. "Here Dan, you better take it now."

Dan replies, "Why? Just leave the stick alone and let the plane do its own thing."

I'm really in for a ride now, and I'd better hold on. With no one at the controls, Dan is going to allow the plane to corkscrew and wander wildly about the sky. But to my amazement nothing happens. The plane just cruises along. Although impressed, I would feel better if one of us had our hand close to the stick, just in case.

"See Mark, the airplane knows how to fly better than you or I. There is no need to fight it, because it has a natural built-in stability. Engineers design planes to fly hands-off. Planes won't just tip over. It requires effort on the pilot's part to make a plane do anything but fly straight and level. And the best pilots use the least amount of control movement. You should only use light pressures on the control stick to ease the plane in the direction you wish to go. The smoother, the better, that's how airline pilots do it. They maintain the smoothest flight possible so as not to spill drinks or upset the flight attendants. Now try it again, but this time with just one finger on the top of the stick, and relax!"

I guess he's right. During his little speech my plane flies straight ahead, all by itself. I suppose if I were an aeronautical engineer, that's how I would design airplanes. Safety and stability would have to take priority over all other considerations; otherwise one's engineering career would be rather brief. As this concept sinks in, I realize that airplanes really can be docile and well behaved.

Taking a deep breath to prepare myself, I place a finger on top of the control stick to experiment. Working the controls more smoothly allows me to gauge the airplane's reactions. Gently I draw the stick back to see how the plane responds. We pitch up, and I can feel my body become a little heavier. Then gingerly pressing forward on the stick, the plane's nose falls, and my stomach immediately responds to the sinking sensation.

Next I ease the stick side to side to see the effects on roll; bank right, then bank left. Next I give the rudder pedals a slight shove with my feet to experience yaw; nose right, then nose left.

Dan coaches me on the coordinated use of the rudder and ailerons. For a properly executed turn, he tells me to push on the right rudder pedal as I ease the stick to the right. He demonstrates that using too much, or not enough rudder, will cause a skidding sensation. A well executed turn results in no side forces whatsoever.

Learning a new skill takes effort. After ten minutes, I can feel fatigue setting in from my concentrated focus on flying the plane. Dan senses this, and offers to take back the controls. In no time at all flying the plane has become simpler, and my nervousness subsides. It is fun learning how to operate the controls, but it's also nice to relax and enjoy the ride.

Before I know it, Dan has us circling 700 feet above a country diner next to a two lane highway. I'm surprised at how quickly I'm adjusting to our height, without the apprehension I had earlier.

From way up here I can smell the greasy odor of grilled hamburgers wafting from the restaurant below. Across the highway from the diner is a big patch of gravel where a number of cars and big rig trucks are parked. Beyond is a large picnic area with tables and a grassy section bordered by Oak Trees.

Through the intercom I hear Dan say, "You hungry? This place has the best burgers around."

My stomach is really too nervous and excited to be hungry, but I decide to go along. "Where're we going to land? The highway's too busy, and there's no runway."

"We don't need no stinkin' runways. I'm hungry!" Dan announces with a phony Mexican accent.

He chops the throttle and I lurch forward in my seat as we descend rapidly over the road. The engine is silent and the propeller casually freewheels as my mind flashes through a scenario of playing chicken with an eighteen wheeler.

I look down the highway for prospective hazards when Dan banks the plane sharply to the left. The world tilts on its side as we gyrate around. Then we roll level pointed at the picnic area, and before my senses can catch up, Dan swoops down over the tree tops. We line up on a grassy patch along side the picnic tables as a dark green blur streaks by beneath my feet. I instinctively lift my legs fearing we may snag a tree branch.

There are some families gathered around those picnic tables who are about to get a big surprise! We plunge down past the trees and round out for a soft touchdown on the scruffy green and brown spotted lawn. Bouncing along for just a moment, we coast by some wide-eyed children eating on a bench to our right. Dan squeezes the stick mounted handbrake to slow our landing roll.

In one motion he turns off the intercom and flips the motor's kill switch. The propeller sweeps to a halt as we get out of the plane. My head is tugged back into the cockpit as I have forgotten to take off my headset. I struggle to keep my hands from shaking as I try to appear as calm as Dan, but it's hardly fair because he's probably done this a few hundred times before!

Just as the first of the curious leave their picnics to approach us, Dan quickly turns to me and says, "You finish securing the plane, and I'll go order us some burgers. Don't be too long!"

I get the feeling Dan doesn't want to stay and play twenty questions with the small crowd that is gathering, so he's decided to ditch me. But that's okay; I don't mind sharing my "vast knowledge" with the interested onlookers. Proud of my machine, I gladly answer their many questions.

Once everyone is satisfied with my explanations, I walk across the highway and into the diner. Feeling akin to a celebrity, I stroll by a few onlookers eating their lunch to find Dan half finished with his burger, and mine sitting at the other side of the table getting cold. Dan found us a spot next to the window, which is all the better to keep an eye on my precious baby.

I sit down and prepare my burger with the necessary flood of obligatory ketchup. The waitress stops by to see what I'd like to drink, and she notices our pile of gloves and scarves on the table, as well as our bulky flight suits p lled down around our waists. "So where did you guys d ive in from?" She asks. "What's the matter, did your rig's heater go out?"

"Well actually, our rig's air conditioner is stuck on full blast!" Dan points out the window to my plane sitting in the picnic area across the highway.

Amazed, the wide-eyed waitress looks back at us. "You guys flew in on that? Wow! I guess that would get a little breezy."

She heads off to get me an iced tea as Dan takes another big bite from his burger. I add a pool of ketchup to my plate in preparation for the large wedge cut fries. Unsure if Dan will be able to pause long enough from his burger, I say, "Man, that hawk was amazing. At first I was so nervous flying, but after you showed me how stable the airplane was, I was able to relax. It's still hard for me to deal with all three dimensions at once; I can hardly walk and chew gum at the same time! Do you really think you're going to have any luck teaching this old dog, new tricks?"

After a strained swallow Dan responds, "I reckon, but it's going to be up to you to read some more books on aerodynamics, weather, regulations, and stuff. There's a lot to learn and there's a lot to practice. I think you'll do fine, and if you make good progress we'll have to get you some floats for the summer."

Dan was right about the burgers here; my first taste was most delectable. It was a hand made patty of fresh ground beef, not the usual frozen slab you find at chain restaurants. "Floats, is that what I saw in the back of the hangar? It looked to me like four big pontoons or kayaks stacked in the corner."

"When the weather turns warm, Rich and I install our floats. We like to fly out to the Delta waters to do some exploring and swimming. Float flying is a blast! It opens up a whole new world for sport flying."

"That sounds fun, but how do you takeoff and land the plane with the floats on?"

Dan explains, "The floats have retractable landing

gear, they're amphibious. With the pull of a lever the wheels go up for water landings and release the lever and the wheels are down for land operations. But the best part of float flying is our annual trip to Lake Monticello. Every August Rich and I go up there to enjoy the excellent flying, clear blue waters, and the warm sunny days. Everywhere you look is gorgeous scenery and wonderful wildlife. We camp under the stars on an isolated beach. The trip is four unforgettable days with not a care in the world, heaven on Earth. So beautiful, it's hard to imagine!" .

I have never been to Lake Monticello, but know that it is north, not far from the Napa Valley wine country. It is the sort of place you see photos of in coffee table books and calendars. It is a secluded pristine lake, and by all accounts, it's gorgeous. To be able to join Dan and Rich on their trip would be fantastic, but the preparation required in the relatively short time would indeed test my limits of learning.

Forgetting my burger for a minute I ask, "Do you think you can get me ready in time to make the trip?"

It is hard to believe how fast things are moving. At first I just wanted to learn to fly, but now I want to learn to operate on floats too. And to top it off, in a mere six months, be ready to take on a trip to Lake Monticello.

Dan works his last big mouthful of burger and gives me a prolonged stare, sizing me up. Finally, he replies with a pensive, "Maybe, just maybe..."

Chapter 7
Higher Learning

The trick, apparently, is to distribute the weight evenly so as to avoid pressure points. Astronauts often comment on the comfort of floating in the weightless environment of space; no pressure points. This lounge chair performs flawlessly, it makes me feel weightless. Or maybe it's the margarita.

This morning was thrilling. After four weeks of learning the basics; turning, climbing, descending, and many takeoffs and landings, I flew my little plane solo for the first time. After a series of practice landings in the early light Dan announced there was no reason to put him through any more punishment. He asked to be let out of my plane and suggested I go do landings on my own.

Takeoffs are relatively simple. After the airplane is lined up on the runway, smoothly advance the throttle. Use the rudder pedals to steer straight ahead, once flying speed is achieved; gently pull back on the stick, and the plane lifts off the ground.

Landings require a little more practice, but are not as difficult as I once feared. First, set up a stabilized descent toward the runway. Control the airspeed and glide path with the throttle and elevator control. Just above the runway reduce the rate of descent by lightly pulling back on the stick, and then reduce the throttle. Compensate for any crosswind by banking into the wind, and use the rudder pedals to yaw the plane so that it touches down with the wheels aligned with the runway. Land with the nose wheel raised, and the plane pointed straight.

Any pilot's first solo flight is reason for celebration. Mine is even more momentous because of the obstacles I have overcome to achieve this goal. Jennifer requires little motivation to entertain, and since this is also Memorial Day, a barbeque seemed in order. Now at day's end, Dan and I are left to relax on my back patio and enjoy the sight of big billowy thunderheads firing off spectacular flashes over the distant Sierras.

With Rich and his family departed, Shannon retreats to help her mother clean up in the kitchen. Dan and I witness nature's impressive fury as we sip margaritas and allow dinner to settle. "Hey Dan, what would happen if a jetliner flew through one of those thunderstorms?"

"The one type of weather that all pilots take seriously is thunderstorms. They can really be hazardous. Fortunately there have been big advances in detection and avoidance of severe weather. Airline pilots have both airborne and ground based radar and satellite images to help plan their course. And air traffic controllers now have improved weather radar. This can be especially helpful in directing aircraft away from the storms."

"I've read about a number of incidents of wind shear affecting airliners. Is that still a concern?"

"Wind shear can be a serious by-product of thunderstorms. It's the sudden change of wind direction and velocity. A new type of Doppler radar has been installed at airports around the country to provide detection. Also, airlines have a training program for pilots that simulate encounters with wind shear, and how to escape it."

I ponder this a moment while I savor the perfect blend of margarita and salt. I like my margaritas on the rocks. Jennifer buys a special margarita salt to apply to the lip of the glass. With each sip I try to get just the right amount of salt granules to roll on my tongue and mash between my teeth. "What if lightning hits a plane?"

"Lightning strikes aren't too dangerous. I know it sounds scary, but if an aircraft is hit, it causes little or no harm to the plane and its passengers. I've seen the effects of lightning strikes, and all it amounts to is a small pitted area in the aircraft's metal skin about the size of a dime. Planes are designed in such a way that every metallic part is wired together to allow the flow of electricity to exit through static discharge wicks located on the wings and tail. And if you are flying at night, you may see flashes of lightning which are originating from great distances. These flashes can appear to be very close, but are often the result of being reflected through the clouds."

"Yeah, I think I've seen that once or twice riding in a jetliner." I add. "The flashes make it look like you're right in the middle of the storm."

Jennifer comes out with a fresh pitcher and offers refills. "Are you two wing nuts ready for more to drink? Too bad Rich had to get going; they're sure a fun family. It was nice of them to give Amelia a ride home. She sure enjoyed herself today."

Dan smiles at Jennifer and points half way up his glass. "Only a little bit, Mrs. T. I have to drive home soon."

I should still have enough salt on the rim of my glass to go along with a complete refill. "Thanks honey, I'll have some more. Jennifer, why don't you join us?"

"I will. I just have to put away a few things and start the dishwasher."

With dusk settling in, the storms over the Sierras really begin to put on a show. A chain reaction of lightning rolls from one end of the line of thunderstorms to the other. The bolts aren't visible, but the huge anvils are lit up like nuclear bomb bursts in the gathering darkness. "What about other types of clouds?" I ask. "Are some worse to fly through than others?"

Dan replies, "Flying through clouds in a jetliner is kind of cool. Layered stratus clouds are smooth to fly through. Most of the time you won't feel any bumps at all. When flying through cumulus clouds you normally feel a bump or two when entering and exiting the cloud. That's because cumulus clouds often have updrafts, and the plane will bounce up a little when flying through these puffy looking clouds. Another cause of turbulence is the change in air density. Clouds are a little colder than the surrounding air, so the air density is different."

"Can't ice build up on the wings if it's too cold up there or if a plane flies through snow?"

"Flying in snow is no big deal. And all the jets have anti-icing systems to protect the windshield, wings, tail, engines, and other surfaces from ice. These anti-icing systems use electrical heaters or hot jet engine bleed air to keep the ice off the aircraft."

"What about heavy rain? I've heard that heavy rain can mean turbulence."

Taking another long sip of his drink Dan replies, "Man you're full of questions tonight! Turbulence is associated with the heavy rain of thunderstorms. Radar uses rain drops, not clouds to reflect its beam to display precipitation. Pilots usually give thunderstorms a wide berth of at least 20 miles. If a thunderstorm is near the airport, takeoffs and landings are delayed until the thunderstorm dissipates or moves away. Thunderstorms typically travel across the ground from 10 to 30 mph, so if you just wait a little while the storm will safely move off the airport."

"Dan, I know that convective turbulence is caused by hot air rising from the sun heating the ground. I heard that another type of turbulence is caused by different wind currents in the sky. Wind flowing over obstacles such as mountains can also cause turbulence like water flowing in a river creating eddies. I think we experienced some of that on a smaller scale when we were landing downwind of the Willow Trees at Dreamland."

"Yeah, there is a common type of wintertime turbulence called mountain wave. This is produced downwind of large mountain ranges when the jet stream is at a lower altitude. The air mass in the mountain wave will flow up and down a little bit like swells on the sea. This can cause turbulence, and is typically found east of the Rocky Mountains. Weather forecasters are good at predicting this type of turbulence because it is easy to track the location of the jet stream. Pilots may change their route or cruising altitude to minimize the mountain wave's affects."

Having another sip of my drink and a lick of salt I say, "I used to worry that pilots might lose control of the plane in turbulence. But now that I've learned how to fly through the bumps, I can see that the plane is stable and really isn't difficult to control. What about the higher winds aloft?"

Dan replies, "Turbulence can also be caused by shifting wind currents in the sky. When you transition from one wind current to another, such as crossing a front, the air can get stirred up. Planes flying through these transition areas will normally experience some turbulence. Again, it may be annoying, like your questions, but not dangerous," he says with a grin. "Man! With all of these questions I'm going to have to start charging you for personal tutoring!"

Just then Jennifer returns with a drink of her own and interrupts, "How about I get you another margarita as payment for Mark's lesson?"

"Okay, twist my arm!"

*   *   *

Despite the many things that Dan taught me before soloing, there is still much to master. I have to learn how to handle the plane in all conditions and circumstances. One maneuver that is critical to learn is the stall. I have come to understand that stalls have been a factor in a number of small airplane crashes.

The term "stall" doesn't refer to the engine, but the wing's lift. For a wing to create lift, it must be angled upward compared to the oncoming relative wind. As this angle is increased, the amount of lift created by the wing increases as well. But once the angle becomes too great the air can no longer flow smoothly over the top of the wing, and it begins to burble and separate. At this point the amount of lift generated by the wing falls off dramatically and the wing stalls.

Stalls are encountered when a pilot neglects to maintain enough airspeed and must pull the nose of the plane up for more lift. Once a stall occurs, the nose of the plane drops, and you have to let the speed build back up to regain the lift. This requires some altitude.

Dan has told me that jetliners fly at speeds that allow for large safety margins. He says the planes are equipped with many alert signals and safety systems. When approaching a stall the jet's computers will sound alarms, flash lights, shake the control stick, and even push the stick and throttles forward if necessary to prevent the stall.

In my little plane I have none of these artificial warnings, but I've learned to recognize the onset of a stall through practice. When approaching a stall I can feel the breeze on my face diminish as forces on the control stick become lighter. I can also feel the burbling of airflow over the wings from the small rumble transmitted through the airframe.

Before my flight training I would have considered such flight maneuvers frightening, but now I am able to handle them with confidence. Taking it one step at a time and thoroughly educating myself has enabled me to handle these drills with composure, though the first few times certainly tested my moxie.

Over the next couple of months Dan teaches me other advanced maneuvers such as spins, spirals, and engine out landings. Occasionally Rich joins us to fly along side during my lessons. This experience helps teach me about flying formation. It is challenging to stay close to another airplane, relatively motionless, while operating in the three dimensional environment of the sky. Steady concentration and focus on the other airplane is necessary, and making gradual flight control and throttle adjustments is essential.

After being introduced to these advanced maneuvers, I spend much of the remaining spring and summer months practicing on the weekends. One important and challenging thing I work on is engine out landings. These practice sessions help build my confidence in the ability of the airplane to glide in a controlled manner while idling the engine to simulate an engine failure. I used to worry that if the engine quit the plane would plummet to the ground. But now I know that gliding is a natural part of any flight, and even large planes fly just fine with the engine off.

Up at altitude I throttle back to idle to become accustomed to how the plane handles in a glide. I pick out a field or a road as my emergency landing strip. Then I judge my descent so as to land exactly where I have chosen. An important variable I have to account for is wind speed and direction. Without a windsock available I have to learn to estimate the wind by other means.

I carefully observe the effects of the wind on blowing trees, grass, smoke, and dust. I also learn to read the wind's effect on a body of water, noting the size and orientation of waves. When flying out in the open, your natural senses come into play to help make up for the lack of instrumentation.

*   *   *

With the onset of warm weather it is time to install floats onto our planes. I have fallen in love with float flying; it is the smoothest flying out there. The air above a body of water is usually very stable. When flying over water, there is little convective turbulence because the surface below is heated evenly by the sun. The plane will just buzz along, steady as a rock!

A plane with floats installed handles just about the same in the air as a plane without floats except there is a little more added weight and aerodynamic drag. The real trick to float flying is the water taxi. Maneuvering a float-plane on the water around boats and docks can be challenging. When there is a breeze the plane will weather vane, or point into the wind. Thus, the planning of the taxi and docking should be thought out ahead of time.

With August approaching, the three of us prepare for the annual trip to Lake Monticello. I have worked hard spending all my free weekends and evenings learning everything I can. I feel a great accomplishment to have come so far, and I am looking forward to using my new skills on our upcoming odyssey.

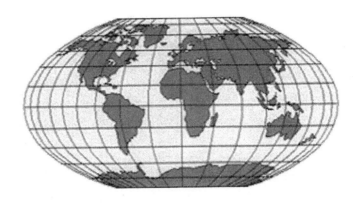

*T*he glorious August sun is shining from the east and beginning to reflect brightly against the large white hangar as I pull into Dreamland just after dawn. The vibrant blue sky gives way to neon green cornfields which form a natural enclosure around Dreamland. The property's once visible fence line is now concealed by the maturing crop.

We have been preparing for this trip for some time and now the big morning has finally arrived. Rich is busily packing his plane with gear for the trip while the CD player blasts the song "Danger Zone."

Dan and Jetlag arrive not long after I do. As the resident expert mechanic, Dan does one more quick check of our plane's engines and fuel systems. He makes sure all of the fluids including fuel are topped off, hoses look good, and cables are adjusted properly. The planes are serviced and in tip top shape for the long flight. All systems are go!

A lot of time has been invested in locating light weight camping gear, much of it purchased from a backpacker's outfitting store. Space and weight are both at a premium. The Dacron fabric wings have large zippered openings near each tip where we stuff our bulky sleeping bags and pads. Most of the rest of the equipment is carried in a duffle bag strapped into the right seat.

We each have small hand held aircraft radios installed in our planes, and simple GPS receivers for navigation. We carefully enter the destination's latitude and longitude and double check them against one another. The GPS will display distance, direction, ground speed, and wind information.

I have spent the last six months learning to fly with

Dan acting as my mentor. It has been an intense process of studying and practical learning. It has also involved a good number of hours out flying on my own, becoming comfortable with my plane and the changing sky conditions.

There were a few times Jennifer and Shannon would fly with me. They really enjoyed float flying. I'd pack a picnic and take Jennifer out to find a secluded little island on the Delta. We would have a nice lunch and lounge in the sun then we'd takeoff and skim along the surface sightseeing and studying the Delta's wildlife. I delighted in sharing the experience with her, and she liked it when I would perform thrilling swoops and dives. Unlike me, she enjoyed the feeling of being out of control. Jennifer was like a kid on an amusement park ride, and I got a kick out of her uncontrollable screaming and contagious laughter.

When Shannon went with me she was more interested in how to fly the plane. I taught her how each control worked and what the instruments were for. She listened very carefully and caught on quite fast. Once when we stopped at a marina for fuel she took the time to answer the attendant's questions with a proud and confident style. Flying really seemed to build her self-esteem.

Unfortunately the girls couldn't accompany me on this trip. I would have loved for them to come along, but there's no room for a passenger with all of the gear I have to carry. They did make me promise to tell them all about the trip once I returned.

Amelia, with a blissful expression on her face, came out to see us off on our voyage to Lake Monticello. She seems so at ease and content today. Maybe it's the bright morning sun that is making her skin glow or she is just excited for us. She carefully looks over our planes inspecting how we have them packed full of gear. She checks that we have everything we need, and is impressed with how efficiently we have planned to avoid taking any unnecessarily heavy equipment. It is interesting though, how she pays particular attention to my GPS. Under her breath I hear her murmur, "If only I'd had one of these..."

A wispy puff of air from the west gently bows the top branches of the Willow trees. Before we leave, Amelia wraps us each in a big warm hug, wishes us luck, and bestows a motherly warning, "Make sure to watch those Delta breezes! I'll miss you guys, have a grand adventure and don't get lost out there!"

In the last few months I have learned what the Delta breezes are all about. We live near the Carquinez Straits, a gap in the coastal range mountains where the Delta waters empty into the San Francisco Bay. During the hot summer months the warm Sacramento Valley air will rise and is replaced by a rush of cooler air from the chilly waters of the Bay. The winds whip through the straits and have a cooling effect on the entire Delta region.

Unfortunately our lightweight planes are susceptible to strong winds. Flying or taxiing the planes on the ground is more of a challenge when the winds are howling, but so far today the winds are light.

I feel a growing sense of camaraderie and excitement to be on our way. With all of the preparation about complete, Rich changes CDs to play one last song, "Born to Be Wild", by Steppenwolf. He turns up the volume and the words echo from the hangar, *Take the world in a love embrace... We were born to be wild, we can climb so high, I never wanna die!*"

With the three engines purring to life we slowly taxi our heavily loaded, fuel laden planes toward the far end of Dreamland's runway. We anticipate a long roll to gain the necessary speed to lift these hefty birds off the ground. With Jetlag at her side, Amelia gives us a pleasant parting smile and crisp proud salute as we slowly parade by.

During the taxi I check the GPS strapped to my left leg. Before launching I want to make sure the receiver has initialized and locked onto at least three of the low earth orbit satellites it uses for positional reference. It's amazing to think that this little black box with four AAA batteries is capable of interfacing with space.

Next, I check the volume and squelch on my two-way aircraft radio. About that time I hear a crackle over my headset and Dan's voice query, "This is Blue Leader, is anybody on yet?"

I look over and see Rich press the transmit button on his control stick, "Roger Blue Leader, Big Sky is now on the air and reads you loud and clear!"

Trying my radio, I key in, "Loud and clear here too guys. Hey what's my call sign? Can I be Red Leader?"

Rich responds, "Negative Mark. We already have a leader. We can't have two leaders. Why don't you be Tweety Bird?"

What does he mean, Tweety Bird? It takes me about two seconds to realize that he was referring to my red colored plane and its big yellow pontoon floats that made it look like the cartoon character of the same name. The other guys had older white floats. The call sign Tweety Bird doesn't sit well, so I ask, "Ah, guys, are you sure, Tweety Bird?"

As we are about in position for takeoff on the grass strip, Dan replies with a chuckle, "That's a big ten four on the Tweet handle. Now are you guys ready yet?"

We take off one by one, Dan, Rich, and then me. Right away I could see how it is going to be on this trip. I am the new guy, and I guess it's to be expected I will have to endure the majority of teasing.

The takeoff roll is prolonged and the climb out is gradual. It is a good thing we are getting under way early in the day before the hot thin afternoon air robs our planes of performance. We are each wearing multiple layers of clothing. The morning flight will be chilly, but later in the afternoon when we arrive at the lake it should be nice and toasty hot.

Climbing and climbing, we slip high over a vast freeway with an enormous traffic backup. Long columns of cars stretching as far as I can see are headed for the urban centers of the Bay Area. I take pity on those poor souls struggling for each inch on their way to a monotonous Monday morning existence. How can they endure such pain day after day? They are far braver than I.

Interrupting the constant whirr of the engine my headset crackles, "Okay let's fly a tight formation and we'll level at 1,000 feet. Big Sky, if you have your camera ready why don't you take some shots of our planes as we climb with Dreamland framed in the background."

Rich replies, "Roger Blue Leader. Tweety, how about tucking in under Dan's left wing and I'll get a shot of you guys with the sun on your right."

I reply, "Wilco Big Sky. Okay Blue Leader, hold steady and I'll join up on you."

With obvious confidence is his plane's stability, Rich releases hold of the control stick and aims his new digital camera as I ease as close as I dare to Dan's plane. As lead plane, Dan just flies and looks straight ahead. As wing man, it is up to me to maneuver over to Dan. In formation flying only one plane should make adjustments to avoid overreactions.

Lake Monticello is almost directly north of Dreamland, but our flight will take us a little east to skirt Travis Air Force Base. Travis, about the half way point for us, often has large C-5 and C-141 transport planes as well as KC-10 tankers which circle to practice takeoffs and landings.

As our small squadron proceeds northward, the wind from the west gradually increases and becomes colder. Evidently the Delta breezes will indeed be a factor for us today. Just as when swimming across a river with a swift current, we find our planes pointing into the left crosswind to keep our ground track straight ahead. And as the crosswind strengthens, our forward ground speed diminishes.

It is fortunate that we had elected to dress warmly this morning. Now with the stronger crosswinds our range also becomes a concern. We had flight planned for an adequate fuel load to get us safely to Lake Monticello, but according to the latest GPS readings that margin of safety is shrinking rapidly.

Our initial plan is to fly at an altitude of 1,000 feet around the Travis airspace, which is well below the 2,500 foot traffic pattern of their large jets. So far this morning, looking out ahead, we see no one in the pattern.

With the Delta breezes eating into our fuel range, Dan announces over our radios, "Hey guys, I think we better try climbing up higher to see if we can get out of these winds."

I keep quiet and let these guys figure out what to do since this is my first trip. Rich replies, "Sounds good Blue Leader. If we can get up above the inversion layer the winds should be less, and maybe it'll be warmer too."

Summertime inversion layers are common in the Delta. An inversion layer is an atmospheric phenomenon where cooler air is trapped below warmer air above. Normally the air temperature cools as altitude increases, but at night, cool ground hugging breezes can slip into the valley under the warmer air above. One can often see evidence of an inversion layer by observing a narrow brownish band of smog with clean air above. Inversion layers are also responsible for the heavy smog in places like Los Angeles.

Dan adds, "Roger. We'll climb up to 2,000 feet and see what it's like. Let's keep a tight formation and our heads on a swivel for any heavy metal."

In my mind I translate what Dan means. He wants us to fly close together so that we will be more visible to other aircraft, and he also warns us to keep an eye out for any large jet traffic around the air base. Our conversations have been light hearted and somewhat silly until now. I can tell by their voice tones that Dan and Rich are now getting down to business.

Sure enough, as we climb through 1,600 feet, my little plane buffets from the turbulent eddy in the atmosphere caused by the shifting winds. I can feel the air begin to magically warm and I smell a pungent chemical odor. Yuck, a concentrated smog layer! But soon we are above the temperature inversion and the air improves.

Rich says, "Good call Blue Leader, much better!"

At 2,000 feet I begin to feel tiny sitting out here in the open with the ground much farther away than I am used to. But Dan is right, without the strong crosswind my GPS shows the groundspeed has increased back up to fifty miles per hour. The air has also smoothed out, smells clean again, and is comfortably warmer. What a difference!

We cruise along with Rich and me concentrating mainly on staying tight with Dan, while our leader keeps us on track and maintains a vigilant traffic watch. With this improved fuel economy, making Lake Monticello will be no problem at all. If we did run low on fuel we would have to find a quiet road near a gas station to refuel. But with the winds whipping up near the surface, landing would present a challenge.

About the time I was being lulled into a relaxed trance from the hum of my two stroke engine, my headset rouses me, "Heavy metal, four o'clock!"

I look over my right shoulder and in the distance just above the horizon is a grey colored four engine cargo jet which is pointing directly at us! It's a gigantic C-5 Galaxy, one of the largest aircraft in the world. I quickly return my attention to our formation to check that I haven't slipped too close to Dan's left wing. When I look back over my shoulder, in exactly the same spot, the jet, which is trailing a light brown exhaust has grown significantly in size.

Although we are technically clear of the Travis restricted airspace these jumbo jets fly a wide pattern and we are now transgressing it. This is trouble because these big jets can close in fast. If they are in training their attention may be divided and they may not be spending a great deal of time on traffic watch looking out the cockpit window. Besides, we are relatively small and have no radar transponders for identification.

There is also the tremendous threat of wake turbulence. Wake turbulence is caused by an aircraft's wing slicing through the air. As the wing generates lift there is a high pressure area below the wing and a low pressure area above. At the wing tip the air below the wing tries to circle up around to fill the low pressure overhead. This creates a horizontally oriented tornado effect. The turbulence usually lasts no more than three minutes, and gradually sinks below the wake generating plane's altitude by about 1,000 feet.

Previously, I had experienced wake turbulence first hand flying around behind Dan and Rich. Normally the first indication I would observe would be the smell of engine exhaust. Then my plane would begin buffeting, normally followed by a roll to the left or right. The roll would typically be fairly gentle and not exceed about ten degrees. Planes of the same size do not affect each other too badly, but put an ultralight up against a huge jumbo jet, and it would be the "PUREE" setting on a blender!

My mind begins to race as my headset remains quiet. I begin to hear my breathing as I wonder why Dan hasn't said anything. That jet is closing fast! Is this what it's like for a poor little insect before going "splat" on a windshield?

The massive jet is a little above us so there's no chance to climb now, and we are too slow to try to maneuver out of its way. If it doesn't hit us, we'll surely be shredded in his angry wake. Say something Dan!

Finally, I hear Dan speak in a surprisingly matter of

fact tone, "Okay, he wins. I guess we're going to have to hit the deck. Let's spiral on down. Blue Leader is breaking formation."

To be safe we have to get well below that jet's wake. So we separate and gently throttle back so as not to shock cool our engines. Each of us enters a descending spiral to lose altitude rapidly. It is a controlled spiral that I have practiced before. We fly tight descending turns, careful not to allow the airspeed or "G" forces to get out of hand.

We're going down fast, but with the plane's high lift wings, still not as fast as I would care to. With each revolution I see the growing jet bearing down on us! The constant turning makes me dizzy, but I focus on my airspeed and altimeter instruments. We follow Dan all the way back down through the inversion layer into the windy, chilly air below. But he doesn't level there, he continues downward. How far is he going to take us? He hasn't lost control or consciousness has he?

Down and down he leads us, my ears popping on the way. Dan levels off just a few feet above the ground. At first I am startled when the jet's shadow flashes before us, but relieved to know he is well above. I have tried to be a good wing man and follow along, but I can't help asking, "Ah, Blue Leader, what's the plan now?"

Dan replies, "How about a low level, terrain following profile? It looks like we're going to have to resort to plan B. I saw more than one heavy metal up there, so we'll have to stay down here for a bit. If we hug the surface we can duck under a good amount of the wind, and hopefully save some fuel."

I have read about surface friction's effect on the wind. As you get closer to the ground, the wind speed will usually decrease. We knew the wind was bad up at 1,000 feet, so Dan's new plan was to fly just above the ground to lessen the wind's effect. It would be bumpy, but as long as we stayed clear of any large obstacles upwind of us, it shouldn't be too bad. This idea might just get us to Lake Monticello without having to try to find a refueling stop. Besides, it was kind of fun.

We no longer fly a tight formation, but a low level line of follow the leader. Leaving the fields of corn behind, we traverse over marshes and rice fields. Then we skim over rolling golden colored grassy hills and occasionally pull up to clear barb wire fences. We stay away from any large buildings or trees that are upwind of us, and we keep a careful eye out for power lines. The trick is to look for the poles that carry the power lines. It might sound dangerous, but at a ground speed of no more than forty miles per hour, there is plenty of time to see the upcoming dangers, I hope.

At one point we happen to fly over a den of coyotes. One of the coyotes must think we are after him, and he takes off running right out in front of Dan. He runs and runs, up one small hillside and down another. With the wind slowing us it is a fairly even race, but in a short amount of time that poor coyote gives up and stops in his tracks. He flashes his teeth at us as we buzz just feet over-head, our shadows looming large on the ground. He must think we are the biggest, meanest, noisiest buzzards he has ever seen.

Now well north of Travis and the straits which once exposed us to the cold and wind, the mountains and the dam that harbors Lake Monticello will soon be upon us. We will need to climb.

We shadow Dan as he slowly advances his throttle to begin the lengthy ascension. The long straws of hay beneath lightly wave revealing the fact that the Delta breezes are much gentler here. The sun is climbing in the sky and heating the earth. Hawks ride the rising thermals of air in search of their rodent prey. As I had read and experienced months ago, I knew that convective turbulence is the result of hot air currents rising from the sun soaked ground. We will now benefit from this rising air like the circling hawk. Updrafts will help lift us back up to a higher altitude.

As we approach the mountain pass, I can see we v ill need even more altitude for safety's sake. The landscape beneath is no longer the friendly flatlands we had enjoyed previously. These hills and mountains are covered with rocks and trees. A general rule of thumb in single engine flying is to never be out of gliding distance from a safe landing spot. This rule is especially applicable to our two stroke engines.

Two stroke engines are used in sport planes because of their high power to weight ratios. But in the past they earned a reputation for being temperamental. Much has improved with the later engines, but it is still wise to operate them with skepticism.

Not only do we take advantage of the rising thermals, but there is also lift to be had from the steep hill sides. Wind hitting the mountains is pushed upwards, and we ride the wave of air for even more altitude. How ironic, that now I am finding turbulence helpful, where before I feared it so.

Up and up we go. As we crest the mountain pass we find ourselves over a large concrete dam. It has been a long morning flight and the welcome view of the placid blue waters of Lake Monticello thrills us with its breathtaking splendor. Shouts of delight ring out over the radio, "Yeehaw, yippee!"

Chapter 9
Blindsided

*D*an announces, "Blue Leader feet wet."

Rich reports, "Big Sky feet wet."

I wonder what the heck they're talking about when I look up to see they have retracted their wheels into their floats in preparation for a water landing. I squeeze the unlock handle and pull on the retract lever to raise my gear as well. Wishing my call sign sounded more dignified I sheepishly announce, "Tweety Bird feet wet."

One by one we peel off into a steep diving turn swooping towards the inviting glassy waters below. I lose my stomach every time I perform this maneuver, but the sensation is beginning to grow on me. These little planes can be flown like a rollercoaster without the tracks, and I'm the one who gets to construct the turns, twists, and drops!

With the majority of the trip's work behind us it is time to play, but first we need to unload our gear at the campsite. We head across the lake with the sun directly above. The winds are nonexistent and the air temperature has climbed considerably. I look forward to shedding these bulky clothes, donning my swim suit, and airing my toes in the warm breeze. I don't know, I guess there's something I like about flying out in the open with my bare feet exposed.

Lake Monticello lies in a north/south direction and is ten miles long and four miles wide with numerous fingers, peninsulas, and hidden coves. The lake's shoreline has both reddish clay areas and stretches of white sandy beach. Above the shore are oak and pine trees which give off an invigorating essence. During the week there are few boaters to disturb the lake's calm surface.

We prepare to splash down near the beach where we will set up camp. Water landings are simple; first, double check that the gear is up, otherwise you will be in for an unpleasant tumble across the water. Next, set up into the wind, if there is one. Slowly reduce power and speed, and ease the floats onto the water keeping the elevator back to prevent the nose of the floats from digging in. With a light spray of mist to signal your landing, you slide to a swift stop. A little burst of throttle and water taxi the plane to the beach. That's it!

Excited to be here, we quickly unload our planes. We pull our sleeping bags from out of the wings, careful not to drop them into the water, and then set up camp under shady oak trees. Changing into our swimsuits and water sandals, we apply sunscreen, especially to the front of our shins and the tops of our feet. Flying out in the open, with one's legs exposed, sunburns are likely.

Dan assigns the first mission, "With our remaining fuel, we'll fly a reconnaissance sortie around the lake to secure the perimeter, establish air superiority, and then plunder the enemy's supply depot."

Rich confirms, "Okay, so we'll check out the lake and stop at the marina for beer and fuel? Cool!"

"Yeah, I guess you could put it that way."

I add, "Sounds good to me. I'll fly close air cover support."

We give our planes a good shove, and as they drift off we wade into the warm water and jump into our seats. We start the engines and takeoff away from the beach towards open water.

Water takeoffs are about as easy as water landings; slowly add power, and hold the stick back so as not to dig in the tips of the floats and prevent the water spray from chewing up the prop. As you gain speed, ease forward on the stick to level the plane. Permit the floats to get up on step where they will have the least contact with the surface of the water, allowing the plane to accelerate faster. Once you achieve flying speed, gradually pull back and you're no longer a boat, but a happy and free flying machine.

We head north along the shore to circumnavigate a portion of the lake in a clockwise direction. The marina is not far to the south, so it will be one of our last stops before we retire for the day. Dan and Rich weave in and out of every cove flying below tree top level. I do my best to mirror their paths which takes us around tall trees, over jagged outcroppings, and skimming along quiet bays. Following close behind, I am mindful to stay above their altitude to avoid their annoying wake.

A slight ripple materializes on the water's surface from the afternoon's light breeze, but my plane is untroubled by its effects. With all I witness on our tour, I wonder how many other fortunate souls have experienced the same glorious feeling of freedom and grace from a flight such as this.

Before I know it, we are at a quaint little marina. We each set down just outside the 5 MPH buoys and taxi our planes to the fuel docks. Greeting us are a couple of clerks and gathering nearby are some curious onlookers, most of which are retired folks who live at the lake.

All the people we meet are friendly and inquisitive, a id I sense they probably welcome a little excitement to their day. I suspect living here at the lake, although very beautiful, can become somewhat dull over time. As the curious surround the three of us, I feel like we are dignitaries from a foreign land.

Dan and Rich take care of buying the supplies, while I am responsible for refueling the planes. The folks here are helpful, offering to hold our planes steady while we prepare to start our engines. It is a challenge to avoid dock pilings and boats, but we manage to miss everything as we taxi from of the dock.

As we clear the 5 MPH zone, Rich proposes our departure strategy, "Okay boys, it's now show time! Let's takeoff in tight formation and then turn around and head towards the marina and give the folks a little air show."

Rich is the most impulsive of the three of us, and he often thinks up entertaining and silly things for us to do. Rich's spontaneity balances out Dan's methodical personality. Me? I'm just tagging along and trying not to get hurt.

Dan replies, "All right Big Sky, you've got lead."

Rich's plane is plowing through the water in front of us as Dan and I flank on either side. "Blue and Tweet, are you ready?"

Dan's abbreviated reply is, "Yessir."

I echo, "Yessir."

"Okay, easing up the throttle..."

Our propellers rip and tear at the water's spray as our planes churn up a frothy wake. Gaining speed, we each porpoise gently then leap off the water to level five feet from the surface. Rich calls for a banking left turn back toward the marina. On Rich's left wing, wedged near the water, I have no room for error now.

As we roll wings level heading for the marina Rich calls for full throttle. The chorus of growling intensifies with our speed while I tuck as closely as I safely dare to Rich's wing. As if the crowd on the dock can hear him, Rich keys the radio to announce, "Ladies and gentlemen, if you will direct your attention to center stage, I would like to proudly introduce *THE AMAZING DREAMLAND NON-PRECISION FLYING TEAM!*"

A 5 MPH buoy streaks beneath us, and before we risk getting too close to our audience Rich instructs, "On my count, Blue breaks right, Tweet breaks left, and I'll pull straight up. One, two, three... BREAK!"

Out of the corner of my eye I see Rich's control stick slam rearward as he disappears above. At the same time I pound my stick and rudder to the left. The turn's "G" forces weigh heavily upon my body as I whip around and a blur of trees and water whisk by before I have to throw the stick back to the right to roll wings level.

For a brief moment I saw hands waving and faces smiling on the dock below. Heading back out toward open water my heart works to process the excess adrenaline. That was a rush but I am glad it's over. Thank goodness we didn't end up doing anything too stupid. Our impromptu air show director, Rich was careful not to fly too closely to the docks, but I'm sure it still provided some good entertainment for the crowd below.

The intense afternoon sun is beginning to broil the day. We join up in formation to fly out over the lake heading for a secluded site to splash down for a needed swim. With the engines stopped, our three planes float in close proximity. We lash the planes loosely together with rope and proceed to plunge into the inviting translucent water. As I look down, my feet are clearly visible with rays of sunlight streaking through toward the lake's bottom. Swimming and joking and laughing, we cling onto our bobbing planes.

Back up onto the floats, we lay in the soothing sunshine as our planes gently rock in a wake created from a distant boat. I didn't notice until now, but there is a candy Pez dispenser strapped to the nose of my plane. It is a Tweety Bird Pez! The guys must have bought it at the store and secretly attached it to my plane's nose gear bar when I wasn't looking. I can't believe those guys were messing with my delicately balanced, aerodynamically sensitive, flying apparatus! I guess my preflight back at the marina wasn't so thorough.

Without revealing my discovery, I bring up the subject of call signs, "Are you guys sure my call sign should be Tweety Bird?"

Rich sharply replies, "Yep."

"Instead, how about Attack Hawk?"

"Negative."

"Maybe Red Devil?"

"Nope."

"Firebird?"

"Nay"

"Crimson Eagle?

Rich sternly says, "No! You are Tweety Bird. We already told you. You don't get to pick a call sign, you are issued one. Another insubordinate remark and you'll be banished from the squadron!"

I try once more, "Buzzard Beast?"

Dan interjects, "Or how about just calling yourself Babble Beak! Now will you guys shut up already?"

With that command from our fearless leader, silence returns. As the water droplets evaporate off my sun soaked skin, I lay and think of what a great day it has been, both exhilarating and exhausting. I used to be so afraid of flying and now I cannot recall when I have been more relaxed.

My breathing becomes deep as I begin to doze off. All I see is a shade of dark red as the sun permeates my eyelids. Resting comfortably on my floats there in the middle of the lake my mind eases off into a deep dream state. A dream which is somewhat fuzzy, not black and white, but full of vibrant colors and surreal sounds.

In the dream it's a bright beautiful day with a hint of a breeze. I'm with my wife floating about on the ocean in a sleek white boat with tall majestic sails. Enjoying each other's company, we sip wine and soak up the tranquil surroundings. As with most dreams, little makes sense. It shouldn't be of concern, but questions crop up. How did we get out here? Whose boat is this? When did I learn how to sail? Where are we?

Our sunny day transforms to an eerie quiet darkness. The sky becomes an ominous navy blue and the ocean is a pitch black undulating morass. Even the sound of waves lapping on the hull is absent. Drifting about lost and helpless our dread grows, and so does the distance separating Jennifer and I. Nothing is said as we stare off and wonder what will become of us.

Out of the darkness above, we hear the soft sound of feathered wings gently flapping. An extraordinary bird appears and gracefully perches on the railing near the bowsprit. Jennifer and I crawl from the cockpit onto the forward deck to see this magnificent bird up close. It has well worn features with friendly familiar eyes which peer steady at us. Speaking in an aged female voice the bird says, "Mark, are you enjoying your adventure?"

Jennifer looks at the bird in amazement and then focuses her stare upon me. Curiously, I'm not surprised by the revelation that this bird talks and knows my name. "No, we're lost! Where are we? What will become of us?"

The bird narrows its eyes, "Why do you worry so? This is your chance to enjoy your time together."

"But look how far we are from the safety of shore. We don't want to die!"

She answers, "Mark, you needn't concern yourself, for dying is certain. Why do you hold onto your desire for control?"

Frustrated, I say, "But I don't know how to sail."

The bird lowers her head slightly and commands, "Mark, fret not over what MIGHT be, but enjoy what IS. Your imagination delivered you here; now only positive thoughts can save you!"

I ponder what the old bird has said. Could she be right? Do I worry over the bad things that might happen? I should learn to appreciate the moment. I take a relaxing deep breath and think good thoughts. At that instant a gust fills our sail and the boat lists to port. Jennifer and I scamper back to the cockpit as I pull on lines, crank the wenches, and man the tiller. The boat lurches forward with a powerful *swoosh!* The bird takes off and flies ahead as the mighty boat speeds along slicing through the waves. The wind is from our right and the main sail is angled to the left. I hoist the jib and trim it along side the main sail. As the bird banks over to the right, I innately recognize that

I need to tack to the right in order to follow.

Main sail? Jib? Tack? I wasn't aware I even knew what these terms meant; now it is all second nature. I pull the tiller to the left, swinging the bow to starboard. The sails ruffle and flop as the boat's momentum completes our turn. The boom swings over our heads across the cockpit, and with a loud *flop* the sails fill with air once again and we thrust forward. I straighten the rudder and release the jib sheet. Pulling tight on the jib's starboard line, I complete the tack. Jennifer, with her hair flowing in the swirling currents of air, shouts, "Whoa, Mark, you've got this baby flying now!"

"Damn right we're flying!"

I yell up to the bird, "This is a miracle! How could I learn this so easily?"

The old bird wisely replies, "Don't you know Mark? When you dare to dream, fantastic things can happen!"

Realizing now that I know this old bird; I impulsively call out, "Thank you Amelia, this is incredible!"

We follow the flight of Amelia until the wind fades and we drift to a stop not far from a strange tropical island with tall palm trees and a white sandy beach. Dan and Rich are on shore wading in the rolling surf. Sitting nearby is an antiquated twin engine airplane with its motors puffing blue smoke as it patiently awaits the return of its missing pilot. As our boat sits dead in the water, the large bird circles and utters, "Mark, it is time for me to go, I'm probably overdue. I'll miss you, my friend. Goodbye"

Amelia, her wings proudly stretched wide, soars up into the boundless sky. As she effortlessly climbs I feel my sorrow grow and fear return. "Please don't leave Amelia!"

Her feathered head turns back one last time to declare, "It is all right to be afraid, but don't ever let fear prevent you from living and growing."

As Amelia vanishes above I hear Dan and Rich calling out, "Uh Oh. Here comes a boat. I wonder what they want. Hey Mark, your turn to answer the twenty questions! Mark?"

Hearing their voices I slowly awaken from my dream. Confused and groggy at first, the sun rudely glares into my squinting eyes, and I see Dan and Rich sitting on their floats, legs and feet dangling in the water. I run my hands through my hair and splash water on my face to adjust back to reality.

As my eyes blink to regain their focus, a ski boat loaded with a family of three motors up to our flotilla of planes. The father calls out, "Hey, sorry to bother you. We saw you guys at the marina and my son Jake wanted to have a closer look. That was quite an air show you put on. Those planes sure look like fun, but I bet it's hard to get life insurance!"

With a chuckle I reply, "When has insurance ever saved anyone's life?"

"What's that Mister?" The boy asks pointing to the nose of my plane.

"This plane is the world's most incredible and versatile candy Pez dispenser! Care for one?"

Jake's family is amused when they see the toy dispenser, and laughter erupts from Dan and Rich, realizing I had finally acknowledged their juvenile prank. Jake reaches out and tilts Tweety's head back to extract the candy. The family thanks us and motors off leaving the three of us bobbing about.

"You know Mark; I think you've found your calling. You can fly around and give out candy to all of the underprivileged children of the world!" Rich quips.

The sun begins to disappear below the mountains to the west. With the flying day about to end, Dan decides it's time to move on. "Let's don our night vision goggles and head back to base."

From previous sunset excursions we had flown, I

knew that Dan meant we should exchange our sunglasses for the clear lenses of the safety goggles he supplied us from work. Dan, who is surely impressed with himself, referred to them as "night vision" goggles. I smile and mumble, "This is just another example of what a couple of nerds I have somehow gotten myself mixed up with!"

As the twilight sky turns a blackish blue, the first stars begin to appear and we enjoy the tranquility of the lake. Airborne, the three of us playfully chase each other and perform mock dogfights until the creeping darkness makes it necessary to return to camp.

We secure our planes for the night, which entails giving them a good yank up onto the beach. We gather the few sticks and firewood we can find, and Dan constructs a campfire even the Boy Scouts would be impressed with.

Rich pulls out thick Porterhouse steaks he had packed on dry ice and we grill the meet over the fire. With a voracious appetite we heartily eat our mouth-watering feast. After our meal we have a couple of beers and a new dilemma presents itself. What now? With no cable television to force feed us entertainment, how will we make it until bedtime?

It doesn't take long for the three of us to settle in for the remainder of the evening. After the fire dies down, we lay on our backs to gaze skyward at the heavens above. There are constellations to name, shooting stars to tally, and satellites to identify. We begin to philosophically discuss the deepest meanings of various intellectual theories concerning mankind today. I start out with a question for Rich, "Hey Rich, do you remember that first day I met you guys out in the cornfield? You were dropping watermelons on stuff, and you said something that I never quite understood. You said that you thought your life might be at greater risk if you DIDN'T fly. What did you mean by that?"

"I don't really remember saying that. What do you

think I meant?"

Reflecting for a moment I propose, "Well I guess I couldn't understand it at the time, but maybe I do now. If you didn't do something a little crazy in your perfectly logical and structured life you might go insane. When you fly there MIGHT be a chance of dying. But if you didn't fly you would SURELY die from the monotonous existence."

Rich sarcastically quips, "Someone better throw Mark a line, because he's getting in awfully deep!"

With the discussion turning too profound, Dan helps rescue the conversation by changing the subject, "So anyway Rich, you grew up in Montana, why would the sky be bigger there than in any of the other 48 contiguous states?"

I chime in, "Yeah Rich, what's up with that? Why do you guys get a bigger share of the atmosphere?"

Rich goes on to defend his home state and then rambles on in a tangent about the vastness of the universe and his theory about creation. It sounds familiar though, kind of a cross between Star Trek's Star Fleet Command Charter and the Jedi teachings from Star Wars. Once we are satisfied we had solved the meaning of life, we retire to our warm and comfy sleeping bags. It has been a very long day, and I find it hard to believe it all began early this morning back at Dreamland.

My inflatable sleeping pad performs magnificently as it dutifully cushions me from the bumpy ground beneath. The night air is quiet, except for the occasional crackle of the dying fire, and a short distance away sits my faithful plane. I will depend on it to not only entertain me for the next few days, but to deliver me safely home. With everything right in the world, I contently drift off into a deep slumber.

*   *   *

With morning comes the sounds of squirrels gnawing on acorns and finches chirping and dropping twigs onto my tent. I awake to the smell of coffee brewing over an early morning campfire. I stumble out of my tent and fumble to insert my feet into my sandals. As I approach the fire's warmth, I give Rich a grunt and mumble, "Morning, how you doing?"

Rich replies in an all too energetic voice, "All vital systems appear to be functioning within reasonable parameters."

Sitting on a stump close to the fire I moan, "Glad to hear that Rich. Is Dan up yet?"

Rich responds, "Oh yeah, you didn't hear his plane earlier? He headed out to fetch us some breakfast."

About that time we hear the lonely drone of an ultralight's engine in the cool morning air. I peer out over the lake bemused by rays of golden sunburst peaking over the hills to the east. Light begins to scatter through the early morning misty fog layered on the lake's glassy surface. Soon the hazy vapors are split by Dan's arrival in a hushed splashdown. His plane slides to a halt onto shore, and in one continuous motion he steps out of the plane and marches towards us proudly holding a line of gleaming fish.

As we all gather about the fire, we sip coffee and dine on the most delicious and fresh tasting Rainbow Trout I could ever imagine. Apparently Dan is also an accomplished fly fisherman. Fortunately for us he carries a small folding fly rod, and is quite proficient in tying his own flies.

Scraping the pan for the last remnants of trout, Dan describes an exquisite inlet he had discovered that morning while fishing. He says it's a dreamlike setting and is abundant with beautiful wildlife. The waters are teaming with hungry fish, and there are rare birds and herds of deer feeding along the water's edge.

After cleaning our breakfast dishes, and doing a

quick, but thorough check of our planes we mount up to explore the area of the lake Dan had described. Heading northeast we practice our formation flying as the chill of the morning air begins to subside with the sun's ascent. Approaching a fingered inlet, we skim along a shallow grassy shoreline. Submerged logs and rocks can be seen down through the clear bluish green water. A herd of Mule Deer feed on the lush green grass and sip water all along the shore. Nearby is a beautiful Snowy Egret fishing the waters for its breakfast.

Up ahead is a gathering of Canadian Geese feeding and bathing in the shallows. Our progress leads us directly toward the large assembly of geese. As we approach they begin to paddle, and then run on top of the water gaining speed. Flapping their powerful brown and white wings they launch into the air forming a modest sized flock. By the time the geese are airborne and have reached our altitude we find ourselves part of their congregation. The flock's speed matches ours closely and only a few feet from us their powerful wings pump them through the air and their heads bob at the end of long slender necks. I can feel the slight buffet of disturbed air as we trail the flock. I note that one does not want to fly too closely behind these large birds for they occasionally release a terrifying variety of dangerous brown bomb-lets!

We split off from the flock, peeling to the right to explore another finger of the lake. This cove contains grassy, golden colored mounds which form small rambling islands and peninsulas. Many of the humps and saddles protruding from the water have oak trees which provide welcome shade for idle families of deer.

The farther into the beautiful inlet we venture, the more frequent enticing sights appear. Our small planes fly rather slowly, but I wish I could slow them even more to enjoy the stunning scenery slipping by.

With Dan at lead, and Rich and I tucked tightly under each wing, we dip down to skip and skim our floats on the mirrored surface leaving ripples in the otherwise undisturbed water. As wingmen, Rich and I shadow every subtle move of Dan's plane. We weave around the scattered islands in an elegant coordinated ballet with every motion graceful and effortless. My mind is not consciously aware of the control stick's movements, but my plane faithfully reacts to each of my whims and impulses.

The pace of pleasant experiences continues to hasten as I begin to contemplate how this setting is just a little too perfect. It feels so good, I wonder if something bad is about to happen. Just like in the movies when everything seems idyllic, disaster can strike! But I return my focus and concentration to the task at hand. I strive to fly safely and keep the proper spacing from the lead and stay alert for trouble, but I also remind myself to relax and relish the moment.

After we complete a steep bank in concert around to the left we level over a flat part of one particular island, grazing only inches above the grassy terrain. Dan smoothly but smartly pulls his plane upward and tilts his wings over toward a singular ancient oak tree. Flying at treetop level, Dan's arm extends toward the tree with his finger pointing at a large twigged clump which looks like an extravagant nest. As we pass closely by I see a majestic bird with a white head and neck feeding a fish to its chicks. It is our national bird, an American Bald Eagle! These birds were once rare, and are now staging a comeback and inhabiting this beautiful lake.

My eyes widen to mimic my mouth as I peer out at the eagle. Stunned by its glorious presence and strength, I feel a great honor to share the same sky with this fabulous creature. As we pass close by, the eagle pauses to give us a complacent look as if to say, "What big noisy birds you are, how do you ever expect to catch any fish?"

Locked in taut formation, we leave the nest behind

to gracefully swoop downward and sail out over the expansive blue lake. I gaze out beyond my naked toes, wiggling in the breeze before me, at the warm sun glinting off the water. Below is the delicate mirrored reflection of our own magnificent creations, inverted on the surface. If only I could somehow seize the moment's beauty, packaging and preserving it to enjoy forever.

I experience a surreal calmness, yet each of my body's senses is aroused to harvest the morning's brilliance. I am happy witness to the beauty of motion, of nature, and of fraternity. The pure freedom of flight is accentuated by the personal satisfaction and accomplishment of being one with a machine I assembled with my very own hands. A machine I once feared has now become an extension of my every thought and reacts to my every impulse.

What happens next takes me by surprise as I am blindsided by this breathtaking feeling. Tears well up as I fight to focus on Dan's wing only inches away. A flood of emotions rushes throughout, permitting my spirit to be nourished from the splendor. My soul embraces the universe and finds perfection with all that is.

At this particular moment in time, born on wings of discovery, I experience an awakening and conviction of faith. It is no particular denomination or religion, but sheer oneness with all that makes up the universe and everything living.

Chapter 10
Slipping Away

*A*viation can be both challenging and spiritually rewarding. Being a pilot is a never ending learning process. Our dynamic and fluid atmosphere ensures that no particular flight is ever the same. Just like in life, there are always things to learn from our constantly changing circumstances.

In the months that followed the trip to Lake Monticello, I shared my new passion more with my family. As before, Jennifer joined me on some fun flights, and when Shannon had the opportunity, I took her up and allowed her to pilot the plane. Shannon's enthusiasm grew and she even n entioned that she might look into aviation programs at c)llege.

Although I like to think of myself as a fairly accomplished small plane pilot now, something still bothers me about riding on jetliners. Jennifer obtained a bargain airfare for a flight in November, and with Shannon off at college the time has come for the two of us to slip away for a vacation. I'm not too thrilled with the idea of a long flight, but recognize I have to face this fear once and for all.

I now understand much about aviation and weather, but I still need more to help squelch my anxieties. In the weeks leading up to our vacation, memories of my flight last year still haunt me. Maybe it's still a control issue. Will I behave the same? Will Jennifer see me reduced to a quivering mass of fear? I again turn to the internet for help.

There is a great deal of information and advice available online, and this helps me feel better prepared in case a panic attack rears up to assault me on the flight. I put some thought into bringing my favorite reading materials, along with magazines containing calming scenic photographs. I am determined to use the time on the plane in an enjoyable way. I even pack some of my favorite games and snacks; thinking I might as well take this opportunity to indulge myself.

Before our flight I make sure to get a good night's sleep, eat a good breakfast, and lay off the sugar or caffeine which might add to the jitters. I plan to leave early for the airport to avoid any additional anxieties. During our drive "Fly Like an Eagle" plays on the radio and I find myself listening intently to the lyrics despite hearing them many times before.

While at the airport's departure lounge I feel hesitant about getting on the airplane. I recall what Amelia had once told me when she was in one of her philosophical moods. "Living your life is like flying a plane, you must keep moving forward or you will drop. And when you encounter turbulence in life, remember that you are strong like an airplane's wing; you can handle the bumps!"

I find courage in what Amelia had said, and when the airport PA calls our flight I approach the gate agent. As suggested in my research, I ask the agent if I can meet our pilot before boarding.

Jennifer and I board the plane and she heads back to her seat while I seek out our pilot. Our captain, Pete Grissom, is a confident distinguished looking gentleman. I explain to him my anxieties about flying, and he is quite understanding and polite. We discuss the route we will take, along with weather and turbulence forecasts. Next I bring up a specific concern about today's flight, "I guess it's one thing for short flights around the states, but for a flight like this far over water, do you take any special precautions?"

"Yes, there are additional rules for extended over water flights which include the requirement to carry extra fuel. Also, the maintenance checks are more stringent, often requiring check flights before a plane is released. This aircraft is equipped with additional radios including high frequency transmitters, satellite communications, and GPS and Omega navigation. And, we carry additional safety, survival, and medical equipment."

"These engines are held to an even higher degree of reliability than on domestic airplanes." he adds. "Additional pilots work on some of the longer over water flights. And flight plans are plotted with equal time points to inform us of the closest alternates. So as you can see, there are many specific procedures, precautions, and regulations that apply to this flight."

The captain's confidence and professionalism is helpful in calming my anxieties. "Did you know that driving to the airport today you were 9,000 times more likely to be in an accident than you would be riding on an airliner? Someone recently did a study and found that statistically, you would have to fly every day for 22,000 years before being in a commercial airline accident. You see, throughout aviation there are carefully designed layers of protection. That means that many things must go wrong in exactly the correct sequence to cause an accident. And fortunately the safety statistics are getting better all the time."

It's good to see that these guys are just as concerned about safety as I am. As this is the same airline that Dan works for as a mechanic, I ask, "Do you know Daniel Martin? He's a mechanic here."

The captain replies, "Dan from the engine shop? Flies ultralights? I'm surprised he's not dead! Yeah, I've heard of that idiot. He's a worthless mechanic, violated consistently by the FAA, and the company has been trying to fire that moron for years! He's not a friend of yours, is he?"

My legs are suddenly cut out from under me. My world tumbles into a tailspin. So much of what I have learned and depended on has come from my friend Dan; how to fly and maintain my plane, and his telling me how safe airliners are. All that trust is now shattered. There is no way I can stay on this flight. How will I tell Jennifer I want off?

The captain looks into my eyes and bursts out laughing, "I'm joking! Dan's a great guy. I used to go fishing with him up to some nice spots that only he can get to in his little puddle jumper floatplane. He is one hot-shot mechanic too!"

Now feeling somewhat foolish, I am relieved and manage a little laughter too. Just about then, the copilot returns to the cockpit from his outside preflight inspection of the airplane and he runs the *Before Starting Engines* checklist. The pilots complete the checklist in a methodical and professional manner. A flight attendant then enters the cockpit to check if the pilots need anything to drink. The copilot overtly flirts with the young woman, almost on the verge of sexual harassment. She simply smiles sweetly and asks, "Hey Bob. Do you know a pilot's most reliable form of birth control?"

The copilot bites, "No."

"His personality!"

That's good for some more contagious laughter. I thank the pilots for their time, and go back to find my seat next to Jennifer. While waiting for all the passengers to finish boarding I begin to feel anxiety building when I think of the agent closing the door. But as I have learned, I use relaxation exercises to calm myself.

First, I use the deep breathing method. Through my nose I draw in slow deep breaths pushing my stomach outward. I hold it for a couple of seconds, and then quietly exhale through my mouth whispering, "Relax." It is easy to forget just how powerful this relaxation tool of breathing is, and after a couple of repetitions I can feel my stress disappear.

Next, I use visualization; a technique which involves picturing a beautiful experience or setting. This is no problem for me as I think back to my days up at Lake Monticello just a couple of months before. I imagine myself lying peacefully on my floats bobbing in the middle of the serene lake. This keeps me occupied until all of the passengers are boarded and we prepare to depart.

Dan explained how everything worked on these jets, so when it is time for engine start I follow along with what is happening. At this point conditioned air is being supplied by the APU, the Auxiliary Power Unit. The APU is a standby turbine powered electrical generator which also acts as an air conditioner. When the pilots start the engines they shut off the flow of cool air for a minute. This air flow is used to spin the jet engines for starting. Once the engines are started the cabin airflow resumes and is now supplied by the engines.

After engine start, I can hear the roar as we power back from the gate. During power backs the engines are placed in reverse thrust to move the plane backward. I look over at Jennifer as she reads her book with little interest in what is going on.

While taxiing for takeoff I hear noises coming from the hydraulics as the flaps are lowered and the pilots make a flight control check. I notice the wings bounce a little while taxiing. Dan told me this is okay because you want wings that give a smooth ride and flex but don't break. There is a short PA from the pilots and a "Ding" to notify the flight attendants to get seated for takeoff.

Our plane aligns on the runway and I hear the engines spool up as the pilots apply power for takeoff. Rolling along I feel small bumps which are caused by the runway surface and the centerline lights. After a few moments the nose of the plane tilts up, and everything seems to get quieter and smoother as we lift off. I am reassured to know from my own experience that the plane is happiest in the air, that's where it operates the best!

On takeoff I find myself enjoying the feel of the acceleration. These jet airliners have lots of power and can really move. Some people worry that an engine might quit, but as I learned from Dan, engine failures are extremely rare. He said not to worry because as with everything else, the pilots are prepared. Engine failures are practiced routinely in training and the drills are so demanding that if an engine does fail it is easy to just circle around and land again.

The FAA mandates that even with an engine out on the takeoff run, the plane must still be able to lift off, clear all obstacles by a wide margin, and comfortably return for landing. Each takeoff is planned so that if an engine fails the pilots can either have plenty of room to stop, or continue to takeoff safely.

After takeoff I hear the thump of the landing gear and the whine of the flaps retracting. I feel the plane settle a little because when the flaps are raised, it reduces lift and increases the plane's speed. From my talks with Dan I know to expect this. Next I hear another "Ding" and a short PA notifying the flight attendants it's safe to leave their seats.

Armed with knowledge and guidance my fears are slipping away. No endeavor in life is completely secure, but I'm feeling much safer. I have learned about flying and life from my new friends and from experiences on the ground and in the air. I'm happier and fulfilled, no longer dormant. There is no one answer in life, and there is no one destination to seek. To live, we must nourish our spirit and remember to try new things because it is much more dangerous to just stand still. Don't run away from your nightmares, run towards your dreams and attend to your passions.

Looking out the window I see the magnificent skyline of downtown San Francisco with the Golden Gate partially shrouded in fog. As we climb higher and higher we encounter some bumps. Turbulence bothered me the most before, but again, knowledge is my savior. I have learned that it is normal to be concerned about turbulence, many people are, but even strong turbulence is quite harmless. For the most part flying is smooth; after all we are riding on air.

Almost magically, my anxieties fade. I think pleasant thoughts and concentrate on the *now*. I don't think so much about what *might* happen, but focus on what *is* happening. Jennifer looks up from her magazine and smiles at me for a moment before saying, "Mark, thank you so much for this trip. You'll see, you'll be fine and we're going to have a great time."

Her glowing face then shifts to an inquisitive look. "Are you sure Howie and the other birds will be okay while we're gone?"

"They'll be fine dear. Brad and Krystal are good kids. Isn't it funny how they think Howie is part cat? I bet they pamper those birds the whole time we're gone."

"I suppose you're right." Jennifer says before returning her attention back to her magazine.

A wave of grief flows up from my stomach and into my chest as I bite my lower lip to hold back the sting of tears. I gave our neighbor's kids careful instructions on taking care of our adopted parrots. Since Amelia's death late in the afternoon on the day we left for our trip to Lake Monticello, we'd grown quite fond of the creatures. It is comforting to have that little piece of her still with us, but I still miss her terribly. My last memory of her will always be of how tall and proud she stood while saluting our departure that morning.

The authorities never located any relatives or next of kin so Dan, Rich, and I handled her affairs. We looked into having her buried at Dreamland, but decided against it. I knew in my heart it would be better to scatter her ashes high in the sky above, where her soul always yearned to be.

Swallowing hard, I return my thoughts to our vacation. I fumble through my small carry on bag to retrieve our travel brochure. I settle back to read up a little more on our destination, Kauai, *The Garden Island*. Then out of no-where a new concern dominates my mind. I turn to Jennifer startling her out of a mesmerized read and frantically ask, "Honey, you did pack an umbrella, didn't you?!?"

Epilogue

Have you ever been surprised by someone in the dark in your own home? You round a corner and "BOO!" Your heart races and breathing quickens as you fear for your safety. You think an intruder is about to harm you. In the next instant you find, to your relief, it is only a friend or family member. For a split second you perceived a danger, but once you learned more about the danger your fear quickly disappeared.

Many people develop fears as they get older; others have lived with certain fears their entire lives. Many fearful fliers developed their fear in their twenties or thirties. With new families to care for, life itself seems more precious and fragile. Regardless of when fear develops, many who suffer often won't get on an airplane at all, holding them back personally and professionally.

Fearful fliers such as our friend Mark react to a lack of feeling in control, turbulence, flying over water, small spaces, and crowds. Many times fears are caused by a lack of understanding about what to expect. Often these fears can be handled with a little education, reassurance, and guidance.

Learning to fly isn't the only way to beat the flying jitters, but some have gone on to enroll in flight school. Mark was lucky enough to learn his lessons from some new friends and also from his adventures. He may have to continue to work at controlling his anxieties, and he may find himself facing new fears or obstacles one day in another adventure. Maybe now when you see a bird or plane soaring overhead you will look at them differently than before.

Below I have included some questions I am asked from time to time. If you crave more information about the fear of flying please visit my online Fear of Flying Help Course (www.fearofflyinghelp.com). I would also enjoy hearing your comments about Mark's journeys in *Wings of*

Discovery, and please feel free to send me an email about your experiences too.

See you on the flight deck.

Sincerely,
Captain Stacey L. Chance
Email - stacey@wingsofdiscovery.com

Frequently Asked Questions:

Q. Which seat is the safest seat on the plane?

A. There are so many variables involved and the chances of being in an accident are so small that choosing a seat based on safety is tough. There are those who believe it's safer to sit near the wings or in the back of the plane, but there is little evidence that any one area of the cabin is safer than another.

Q. When is the Best Time to Fly?

A. Day or night really doesn't matter to the pilots. We can see fine and we have radar and Air Traffic Control to help us out. Night may be just a little smoother near the ground because you don't have the sun's heat to cause convective turbulence.

As far as what time of year to fly, each season has its advantages. In the wintertime the air is normally smoother during take offs and landings. The air temperatures are also cooler, making the air denser. This gives the airplane added performance.

Springtime signals the end of ice and snow, and temperatures are moderate. One can find the views from above to be spectacular. Spring is the beginning of thunderstorm season, so you might find yourself making deviations around storms.

Summertime means no more de-icing delays and fewer delays due to fog depending on what area you are flying in. The jet stream moves north which means westbound flights will have weaker headwinds.

Fall is probably my favorite time to fly. There are normally very few thunderstorms, and very little ice, rain or snow. The air is generally smoothest during this time of the year with little mountain wave or convective turbulence.

Modern jetliners are far less susceptible to the weather than in the past. The jets can climb quickly up through the weather and cruise above the majority of the clouds. So no matter how dreary and bleak it is on the ground, in just a matter of minutes you can be cruising comfortably above a blanket of clouds in the sunshine.

Q. How often do things go wrong with airliners?

A. As reliable workhorses, jet airliners are not only designed to be safe, but to make money too. The plane's systems are built to last. If they always broke, the airlines would find another plane to use. Boeing and the other aircraft manufacturers know this. Failure of a system or component is rare, and when they do fail there are redundant systems installed. As an example, a common jetliner in use today has three main, but separate electrical systems including an on-board generating system. The plane only needs one electrical system to power everything. Even if all three systems failed, the airplane's batteries would power many of the essential systems until landing.

Q. How does the plane's pressurization system work?

A. The engines draw in fresh clean air and compress it with their turbines. That air is fed into the air conditioning systems to cool it or warm it as necessary. This conditioned air enters into the cabin through the vents located near every seat. At the back of the plane are a couple of outflow valves that regulate and restrict how fast the air escapes the cabin. The entire pressurization system is automated and monitored in the cockpit. If the automated systems fail, pilots normally have control of the outflow valves by manual backups.

Q. Can doors be opened in flight?

A. The doors cannot be opened in flight. The doors act as a plug when the cabin is pressurized. The pressure holds the door tightly against its door jam seal. Upon landing, pressure relief valves make sure the cabin is de-pressurized so the doors may be opened.

Q. Is it true that the radar cannot detect clear air turbulence?

A. Turbulence troubles quite a few people. Doppler radar has made displaying turbulence a reality, although up at cruise altitude we still encounter unexpected turbulence. Rough turbulence is very rare and usually very brief. Turbulence often feels worse to the passengers in the cabin than to the pilots in the cockpit. It is also an issue of being the one who is in control.

Q. I've felt planes slow down after take off. That makes me think something is wrong with the plane and we have to turn around and land again. Why do they do that?

A. Often speed and power changes are required by ATC to fit us in line with other airplanes. We try to do this as smoothly as possible, but this is normal.

Q. I've been on planes that tilted (sideways) so much during the landing I thought the wing would hit the ground before the landing gear.

A. During landings the wings will tilt in reaction to the wind. In response to a crosswind we will tilt the upwind wing downward to keep the plane tracking straight down the runway. These crosswind landings are learned very early on in our basic pilot training.

Q. What are air pockets? Are they just a form of turbulence?

A. Air pockets are actually not a good name. There are no "pockets" of air out there waiting for planes to fall into. Sometimes as we change altitude the headwind may reduce or change to a tailwind, and it feels like you are falling, but it just takes a second or two for the plane's momentum to catch up to the new wind it is reacting to. If the wind change is great enough, we add power to make up for the temporary difference.

Q. My greatest time of stress is during the moment of lift-off and continues maybe 20-30 minutes into the flight. For some reason I'm afraid that the engines are going to blow from all of the enormous strain that is being put upon them during this time.

A. One reason the engines are so reliable is that we only use a portion of the available power during takeoff. The engines are capable of producing much more power, but to reduce maintenance and increase reliability, we don't use full throttle. In simulator training we get to experience just how much extra power is available, and it's impressive. So next time you are taking off, remember the engines are actually taking it easy.

Q. What do you do if an engine catches fire?

A. Engine fires are very rare. However, if we do have a fire there are many ways to fight it. With the pull of the fire handle we can shut off all fuel and hydraulics going to the engine. This starves the fire of combustibles. Then, with a twist of the handle we shoot a fire extinguishing agent all around the engine. Then we wait 30 seconds, and can shoot another extinguisher if necessary.

Q. What if you do fly into a bad thunderstorm?

A. First, we do everything we can to avoid thunderstorms by a wide margin. If we do somehow end up in a thunderstorm we can set up the plane to handle the rain and turbulence. We turn on the backup igniters to ensure the engines will continue to run in the heavy rain. We also fly the plane at the best "Turbulence Penetration" speed. This is the speed which gives us the most controllability, while being slow enough that it guarantees that the plane cannot be damaged by the bumpy air. We fly straight ahead and should be out of the storm soon.

Q. What happens if the plane drops suddenly in a strong down draft?

A. Strong downdrafts are also very rare, and usually very short in duration. If we encounter a "Microburst" downdraft (usually the strongest type of downdraft), we have procedures to obtain the maximum performance to combat the downdraft. We can increase the engine thrust to a "reserve" setting which is greater than normal maximum. And then we use all excess airspeed to convert the energy for climbing. We routinely practice this maneuver each year at recurrent pilot training.

Q. Does one feel less turbulence on larger aircraft, e.g. 747s, than smaller aircraft like 757-200?

A. Turbulence seems to be the number one thing that bothers people about flying. The 747 may be just a little less influenced by turbulence than the 757 but I don't know if it would be worth adjusting your travel plans around.

21203688R00080

Made in the USA
Lexington, KY
04 March 2013